Mr. Nachron's List

"Just in time"

Mike Corbett

Mike Corbett

Centrifugal Publishing

Copyright © 2011 Mike Corbett

All rights reserved. No part of this publication may be reproduced or transmitted in any form or by any means electronic or mechanical, including photocopy, recording, or any information storage and retrieval system, without permission in writing from both the copyright owner and the publisher.

Requests for permission to make copies of any part of this work should be mailed to Permissions Department, Centrifugal Publishing, PO Box 11874, Fort Lauderdale, FL 33339

ISBN#   978-0-9830679-2-4 Paperback
         978-0-9830679-3-1 eBook

Printed in the United States of America

Library of Congress Control Number: 2011922349

ACKNOWLEDGEMENTS

I would like to thank Keely Stahl, Steve Kantner, Michael Mangold, Renee Mangold, Ann Clark, Steve Vaughn, Elysa Lipman and Maureen Buckley for their insight and support throughout this process.

I am very grateful to a talented Fort Lauderdale artist, Frank Zorman, who brought my cover sketch to life. (Silhouette of fisherman provided by Patrick Ford.)

Special thanks to Danielle, whose energy and determination continue to inspire me.

Mr. Nachron's List

Mike Corbett

LEPER SHOOTS LEPER.

No Onlookers in Panama Court When Shooter is Found Guilty.

Special Cable to THE NEW YORK TIMES.

PANAMA, Jan. 29.—Robert Lavison, a leper, in the colony at Palo Seco, in the Canal Zone, was tried this afternoon before Judge Gudger in Ancon on a charge of attempted murder. He shot another leper in the colony in the course of the wedding of two other inmates. The court was deserted by everybody except the officials when the case was called.

Lavison was found guilty, but there was no place to send him, and he was sent back to the colony after a reprimand. The trial was very brief.

The New York Times
Published: January 30, 1913
Copyright © The New York Times

INTRODUCTION

Only a very small percentage of this book can be accurately called fiction. History and science are full of surprising and improbable truths, and it was my intention to connect some of these in original ways. If the result of this effort neither amuses nor enlightens, then it is destined to fail. If just one of these criteria is satisfied however, Mr. Nachron's List will join the huge number of books available that would be valued marginally higher than the paper they are printed on.

I have been repeatedly advised by my publisher and other critics not to overly rely on science, math or the usage of uncommon words, and if I insisted on any of these elements, I was told they should be buried deeply within the text. They challenged me to name a best selling novel that referred to the symbol for pi (π) more than once.

Writing fiction for general consumption is problematic for me for reasons other than the issue of personal restraint. I had never been challenged to speak with any but my own voice and my own opinions. Writing Mr. Nachron's List required me to create characters of both sexes and diverse points of view who didn't all sound like me. Writers with multiple successes would no doubt scoff at my limitations, but the creatures that populate my imagination tend to be grotesque or cartoonlike, not readily lending themselves to credible modern fiction. I addressed this shortcoming by borrowing the authentic characteristics of a number of my real-life friends and acquaintances. I even took the liberty of superimposing a few of my own most obvious flaws onto their personalities in order to make them seem less wholesome. I hope they don't assume I got hold of someone's diary.

Mr. Nachron's List

Mike Corbett

ONE

South Florida

At that moment there was nothing I could see, hear, or smell that did not bring me pleasure. I was, in a sense, the sole possessor of this perfect moment, and I reveled in the selfish comfort that it could not be stolen or even shared without my knowing well in advance.

The sun warmed my bare back to the perfect temperature and the moisture laden air was subtly enhanced by sea smells with a salty tang. The only sounds were the occasional clatter of mangrove as some creature negotiated the woody tangle, and less frequently, the displacement of water produced by an escaping or pursuing fish.

My eyes were partially closed against the morning glare, but I saw my feet quite clearly. They are tanned and very useful feet, so I knew

I wasn't a lawyer or a telemarketer, but as to the specifics of my identity, I had never been more uncertain. There was once someone who I could have relied on to help me with this dilemma, but that person has gone somewhere else, so I was literally and figuratively adrift.

My feet were unevenly spaced on the poling platform of a small shallow-draft boat that I had borrowed from an old friend. I knew that if I left early enough on a weekday morning, I might have a pretty good chunk of the flats west of Elliot Key to myself. There was a long period that little attention was paid to the southeastern part of Biscayne Bay since it was relatively inaccessible and of no obvious use except to its natural inhabitants, but that era has passed.

On my last visit, I poled around the northern tip of the little island from the windward side to witness something I can never hope to erase from my memory. A very large speedboat called "Lady Killer" had either deliberately or accidentally been driven up onto the sand to discharge its contents, a giant pink nude fisherman, onto the shelf. I thought at first that the guy had run aground by mischance and decided to make the best of it. It became obvious however, that he was a tourist who thought grinding up a little bit of the flats under his boat and insulting the view with his naked body was the way we did things in South Florida.

I poled slowly closer to confirm the perplexing vision my eyes had supplied. The guy was wobbling clumsily across the flat with a fly rod alternately producing whiplash cracks behind him and dropping tangled loops of line in front of him.

Although no fish was likely to have fought its way through the snarled web of line he was heaving to get to the fly, I suppose it might have been possible to ensnare a nearly blind one by the gills.

    The relative solitude I enjoyed after this disappointing encounter permitted me to dismiss this vision and replace it with more agreeable memories. When I wasn't hung over, I could pole a boat stealthily across a flat without waking nurse sharks or partially buried rays. It is an art to direct a boat efficiently across the wind with a push pole without pounding noisily in and out of the rock and sand that comprise the flat. Dropping a fly gently, then lifting it with the energy imparted by wrist to an expanding loop and in defiance of the surface tension's grasp on the line, is an attendant art. Redelivering it noiselessly is such a rewarding craft that you really don't need fish to justify the effort. Consequences are secondary to the actions themselves unless you have a starving family.

    I didn't bring a rod with me that day since I knew I would be sufficiently gratified by insinuating myself gently into this environment. The tide had recently replaced most of the water under me and the jets from Miami International hadn't yet begun turning out over the Atlantic. They weren't too distracting even at the busiest hours due to their altitude that far from the airport, but I needed to isolate myself as much as possible.

    As the sun rose fully above the horizon, I heard the sound that would announce not only the end of my perfect morning, but possibly the eventual collapse of civilization as we know it. The first personal water crafts* were leaving their rental docks to invade every navigable inch of the bay and spoil the morning's subtleties with their whining engines. If I wanted to be around excessive noise and speed, I'd go to a NASCAR event, but for the time being I just dropped my little outboard motor back into the water and turned north into the channel for home.

Whenever I noticed the message signal on my phone blinking, I hoped to hear only one voice. The hundreds of disappointments my expectation had produced never discouraged me from the belief that things could again be as they were, but this time, as in all the previous times, it was not to be.

I listened as the heavily accented voice of my friend Michel enthusiastically informed me of his latest idea. Michel, since leaving France fifteen years ago to make his fortune in America, had experimented with one gimmick after another to the detriment of the many investors he had beguiled with his Gallic charm. His latest, according to the unmistakable pride in his tone, was to be the triumph that would earn him a place in history. It

---

* Jet Ski dealerships and rentals are unfortunately growing at a fearful rate.

was, he proudly claimed, the answer to almost all of life's challenges.

He had rented a two story building that was once the hub of Fort Lauderdale nightlife[*] and transformed it into a church. The irregular layout of vaulted ceilings, interior balconies, and excellent acoustics made it seem less preposterous than some of his notions, but there was one significant difference. This church was created to simultaneously provide not only a house of worship, but a place of exercise and weight loss. The rhythmic and passionate preaching, Michel believed, could induce a congregation of the health loving faithful to bounce and stretch in a cardio-positive manner while discharging their periodic obligations of prayer and modest tithing.

He left his phone number with the advice that opportunities like this one would tempt many investors, so I should act quickly. Every time Michel left a message for me to return his call, the number was different, so even if I had some spare cash, I might have hesitated because of his dubious record. That I was even included in the recruiting presentation of this well meaning but self-deceiving capitalist only called my attention to the sorry state of my own affairs. Was this to be my era of self-realization? Was I being captured by my own inertia into the improbable dreams of others? I hoped that I hadn't passed the point where the slippage would become irreversible.

---

[*] Montego Bay, which still stands as a monument to the era, always had a line on weekends

Mike Corbett

"The distinction between past, present, and future is only a stubbornly persistent illusion."   Albert Einstein

TWO

The Present

My name is Ron Maddock, and I used to believe the people who told me that I was special. Although I am composed chiefly of water that has been enhanced by a few other compounds, I dare to imagine my place in a vast universe. If extraterrestrial beings choose to visit earth, the human race may seem no more interesting to them than ducks, horses, or viruses unless the toxic footprint that man has left on our planet is given weighted importance. Perhaps we will be rated according to how much energy we generate relative to our size, in which case a firefly may be a more fascinating subject for study than the CFO of a multinational corporation.

Do I sound like someone who wants to differentiate himself from the rest of the cosmic debris? That will be extremely challenging unless I can depend upon the buoyancy of the supernatural. The obstacles to that aspiration are that heaven may not react to my wishes and hell may not give a damn. I did not deliberately set out on a mission to reinforce my identity, but the opportunity was thrust on me so I embraced it.

I thought I was only one person, but it turns out I was many, and the era to which I believed I belonged was merely one of an infinite number to which I enjoyed equal access. Does this make me special? All the possible responses to that question are relative and dependent on a higher system to prove. Mr. A. Nachron may have been an envoy from some elevated plane, and thanks to him or perhaps in spite of him, I have the courage to believe in something far beyond my intellectual reach. In the following chapters, I will try to show you how this all happened, and that I am not insane.

"Whereof what's past is prologue, what to come in yours and my discharge."   William Shakespeare

THREE

The Past

Having never read an entire book, neither my friend Jeff nor I could have imagined a comparison between us and Mark Twain's charming characters. Like Tom and Huck however, we were not distracted by caution or the guidance of others, so we produced our own adventures, mostly on a ten foot boat that we kept at an oceanfront motel in Lauderdale-By-The-Sea.

Before its eventual theft, we would ride our bikes to the beach in the middle of the night and row to the second reef, where we almost always found mangrove and mutton snappers to sell to the nearby restaurants the next morning. It didn't seem like a big deal to a couple of thirteen year olds until the night our tiny craft, which had no flotation vests or signal lights, and only a flashlight on board to warn off approaching vessels, was nearly swamped by a large pleasure yacht. Both of us could swim the half mile to shore, but there was always the chance that an oncoming boat would swerve at the last minute to avoid the collision and chew us up in the props as we swam to escape. Fortunately, the pilot of the yacht saw us in time to avoid tragedy.

We were never bothered by sudden storms or rogue currents, which we assumed to be fictitious, but there were other hazards. Because of the tiny unlit area in which we were compelled to function, we established a routine that served us pretty well 99% of the time. When one of us would bring a fish into the boat, he would dangle it in the face of the other to be unhooked and placed within an ice chest. We learned to adapt to the circumstances since holding a rod, a flashlight, and three pounds of sharp-toothed snapper requires more than two hands to perform in a reasonable amount of time. This system worked fine until the moonless night my buddy accidentally swung a moray eel into my lap that weighed at least fifteen pounds.

As I tried to squirm away from the nasty jaws, I yelled at him for his inability to distinguish eel from snapper by the way it fought the pressure of the line. I kicked an oar in my panic and it hit Jeff on the shoulder, prompting him to retaliate by swatting me with his rod, which in turn precipitated the brawl that nearly sunk us. We wrestled among the jagged contents of our overturned tackle boxes while the eel thrashed menacingly between us, making the little boat slop back and forth, nearly capsizing. We did more damage, as evidenced by a scar I still have on my back, than the moray could ever have done. We rowed back threatening each other with a resumption of the dispute on the beach, but one of us (not me) was smart enough to propose an end to hostilities.

You just can't do much better than growing up in South Florida. You can easily go south, east or west for a relatively short time and reach international waters. Once there, it's possible to harvest stem cells, practice polygamy or teach evolution without the threat of some authority imprisoning you for it. You are still responsible to the extent that you are guided by international law or personal morality, but for the most part, an individual may set his own course to maturity on such a frontier.

My father died before I turned thirteen, and my mother could not control me and provide for us simultaneously, so I ran wild through my adolescence. I learned how to drive cars and motorcycles before I could legally obtain a license, and alcohol and tobacco abuse were peer-dictated rites of passage. Youthful ignorance produced the illusion that hurricanes weren't dangerous, but merely a temporary end to school and a great opportunity to surf. I'm sure you couldn't keep drunken Iowa kids out of tornados either, but we were fascinated by leaning into the howling winds to see how sharp an angle would support us while garbage can lids and tree branches flew by. Since I've never lived in Canada or Finland, I can't really say if the colder climates somehow deprive their inhabitants of comparable stimuli, but for twelve months a year I could find a place on a beach to have a beer and make love to my girlfriend. How do you top that?

Permit me to make one final argument for seeking the answers to life's many mysteries in the seductive environment of South Florida. There is a special moment between consenting parties who are attracted to one another that can be best enjoyed when accompanied by a first kiss or caress. In order to savor this moment to the extent that nature intended, it is best if you are outside in the darkness, and standing upright. In Pittsburgh's bitter winters, couples are forced to endure the inconvenience of layers of clothing obstructing an awkward crosswise lunge across a dirty car seat.

On a Fort Lauderdale beach almost any time of year, you can pull your partner closer with gentle pressure on the small of her back and brush her bare shoulder with the hand that slowly finds its way to her cheek or the back of her neck. She, in turn, will tremble and wait for the first touch of your lips before pressing her body softly against yours. For optimum results, you should position yourself close enough to the shoreline to hear any sound the ocean is making, and keep the moon at your back so the flaws in your complexion will be hidden. You don't have to worry about these technicalities in Akron in February.

It might seem that someone like me would be too infatuated with the lifestyle to ever leave this sunlit paradise, but I had to prove to myself that I could be carefree and irresponsible in a variety of settings. I don't remember what I studied in college, but I remember what I learned. Along with a pretty fair grasp of three languages, I brought a passably competent knowledge of chess, tennis and backgammon with me to Europe, where I competed well enough to earn a modest living. I became such a regular passenger on the trains from London to Paris, Monte Carlo, Venice, Prague and back that some of the veteran pickpockets recognized me and left me alone.

Study and practice never made me a great player of anything, but I was opportunistic and charming enough to cultivate friendships that have persisted over many years. The one talent that I took pride in was a chameleon-like ability to mingle with the locals. Although I could never completely master the various nuances of European tongues, I was widely assumed to be too peculiar to be American and thus a tolerable curiosity among the worldly.

I eventually returned to Florida where I made a heroic effort to splice the pleasant memories of my past to what I hoped would be a meaningful existence in Fort Lauderdale. I had saved a bit of money in Europe, but other than a rental apartment and a few bucks in the bank, I had little to show for the first decades of my life.

Mike Corbett

"History is the version of past events that people have decided to agree upon."   Napoleon Bonaparte

FOUR

It's difficult to spend a lot of time around Fort Lauderdale beach without occasionally visiting one of the local pubs. By the time I was thirty-five years old and the beneficiary of a liberal upbringing and education, I had dedicated at least half of my waking hours to the various employments and entertainments of South Florida night life. Alcohol wasn't the principal attraction, although it seemed to bridge a lot of the gaps that would have bored most sensible people out into the street. It was the hypnotic combination of subdued lighting, loud music and background laughter. And who am I kidding, it was the girls.

If you know your infant daughter is going to grow up to become a cocktail waitress or bartender, you can save yourself a lot of effort trying to choose an appropriate name for her. You have merely to decide between Tiffany and Crystal (with its numerous alternate spellings), which outnumber traditional names like Ann or Judith by a ratio of eight to one. Potential employers simply ball up employment applications with those other names and throw them away.

    I carelessly lost my wallet one night at the Aruba Restaurant on Fort Lauderdale Beach, where I was served capably by an attractive brunette named Crystal. When I returned the next day to hopefully reclaim my property, I asked the hostess if Crystal had come in yet, and she asked; "Which one?"

    I don't mean to imply that there is some sacrifice of individuality in this apparent coincidence, since my best friend bears that name and I consider her to be very special. Her friendship is one of the reasons I spent so much time at Murray's Pub on Las Olas Boulevard, where she has worked for the last three years. That night, I must have been atypically quiet, because I kept catching her looking at me with a concerned expression on her face. I had been loved and discarded by an embarrassing number of potential mates, but Crystal, with her job-enhanced ability to separate truth from fiction, knew something else was wrong. She sensed that the memory of one person in particular, an amazing girl named Lynn, could thrust me into a reflective state that was totally unnatural, so she poured doubles until closing time.

    Among the many remarkable qualities that Lynn possessed, she was able to see through the artifice and exaggeration that I had deceived myself into thinking was my personality. From what remained, she was able to coax out a functional counterpart to her own versatile, if somewhat quirky nature.

She was a creature of impulse, and her impulses were dramatic and irresistible. Because of my infatuation, I would sometimes not notice that they were also frequently dangerous. I should have guessed how unusual we must have seemed to others by the strange way people recoiled from us when we were together in public, but I chose to ignore signs that normal people might have taken more seriously. When an envious stranger at the adjacent urinal in the men's room says something like "dude, you gotta get her to a motel", you should be alert that life is about to become more eventful.

I was hypnotized by her carefree sensuality, and took for granted that some part of her anatomy was always against my skin. She had probed so often and so vigorously into my pants pockets with her hands that the holes she made enabled her to hook her index finger into my back pocket and touch bare skin as we walked. We never cuddled. We wrapped around and through and into each other until no square inch of flesh was left cool to the touch. A barrel of wet snakes could not have been closer.

I assume all couples behave like this sometimes, but I had never been so keenly aware of how satisfying it can be when you're not taking it for granted.

One night, I walked into the apartment we shared two hours later than I had promised to find her sitting in the dark smoking (something she only did to punish herself for drinking too much). As I entered the room, she expertly flipped her half smoked cigarette into my chest where it exploded in a cascade of embers. When I tried to stomp out the flecks of glowing ash and carpet, she emitted a low feline growl and sprang at me, alternately clawing me, kissing me hard with her open mouth and biting my neck and throat. Whether she was penalizing me for my tardiness or indifferent to it, I couldn't guess, but I could not have been more satisfied. She was attractive, intelligent, and I thought she loved me passionately, so why after two years did she vanish?

In the months that followed Lynn's abrupt disappearance, Crystal and I would swap opinions about our past and future over a cocktail, and one night I detected an odd little well-dressed man who appeared to show an interest in our conversation. We both smiled politely in his direction and resumed our small talk, which thanks to the thin weeknight turnout, continued with few interruptions. At least an hour had passed with the little man stealing sheepish glances in our direction all the while. It felt in no way intrusive, as the guy's demeanor resembled that of a well-trained puppy beneath the dinner table. As Crystal observantly remarked, the little fellow was irresistibly cute, so we simultaneously had the idea of sending him a drink, which turned out to be one of those sugary things that guarantee there will always be ants behind bars. He nodded his head and lifted the colorful drink in a gesture of gratitude, and at that moment, although I was unaware of it at the time, my world had changed forever.

He turned out to be charming and articulate, and I started thinking about how putting down my guard and relaxing a bit might be therapeutic. I learned from his business card that his name, with no claimed affiliation or profession, was Mr. A. Nachron of local residence, but he said his friends called him Albert. It became clear during the next three hours that Crystal was as taken by his disarming personality as I was, since she frequently threw her lovely head back in a girlishly receptive response to his stories.

    Bartenders never go home immediately after closing. Even at 2:00 AM, it is not uncommon for club employees to "wind down" after a shift with a few drinks and maybe breakfast, and since Albert lived within walking distance, Crystal and I accepted his invitation to join him for a nightcap. If you walk a few blocks west from Murray's Pub, you will see a number of apartment buildings overlooking the New River, which winds attractively through downtown Fort Lauderdale. We passed by the valet and doorman at one of those residential high-rises and took the semi-private elevator to the penthouse level, where we settled into his comfortable thirtieth floor apartment. During the next two hours, we were treated to some excellent brandy and a conversation I shall never forget, although Crystal curled up on a couch after an hour or so and swears nothing unusual occurred.

    If I hadn't been drinking, I doubt that I could have been tempted into a conversation about space, time, and relativity with someone I barely knew, but Mr. Nachron's knowledge and imagination were compelling. When he said he might be able to help me learn of Lynn's whereabouts, I was curious. When he explained how he might do so, I was aghast. The following account, as near as I can remember, revisits Albert's comments and how I might benefit from them.

"The universe," Mr. Nachron patiently explained, "is slightly more complex than even twenty-first century science would acknowledge. Humans are comfortable regarding events and the passage of time in a way that suits their sequential perspective and minimizes confusion about possible alternatives. Reality, it seems, is not similarly confined. Light can be bent and even trapped by gravity, the weakest of the basic forces. An electron can exist simultaneously in two locations. Time and velocity are relative and crudely measured. Theoretical science postulates strings, ribbons, and multiverses permitting infinite numbers of observations about the nature of neutrinos and supernovas."

"The thing is," he continued, "Even the broadest perceptions of reality may be myopic. What if I told you that time is neither sequential nor are we hostage to its passage? Not only are you here, in my home, you are in many other places at other times in innumerable settings with unimaginable directional possibilities. You are a cooperative assemblage of tiny particles that have existed or will exist, if you prefer, in any number of configurations on a scale your mind cannot wrap around. Don't be alarmed, it will merely seem to you that you are only here and it is just now."

If I thought I could have wakened Crystal or carried her out on my back, I would've headed for the door. His implausible message was too well-crafted to be a joke, so I deduced that we were in the company of a brilliant lunatic, and my feeling of wonder had begun to be joined by a hint of fear. He must have sensed my discomfort and chose to respond to it by suggesting that I ask a few questions to dispel my doubts.

"Huh," I said. I wanted to construct a tactful challenge to what I had heard, but no single question could address my many concerns, so I asked him to give me some practical application that I could "wrap my mind around".

"Imagine," he began, "that you and your many attributes, good and bad, simultaneously exist in other locations at other times. However, your sense of awareness can only apply to one of these at a time or it could become confusing."

Well, for me it had become confusing quite a while ago, but I persisted. "You mean there are other versions of me rattling around somewhere?"

"Naturally, my boy," he responded, with a creepy familiarity. "At last count, I detected eleven of you in an eighteen hundred year survey; a relatively small number. There are, by way of contrast, almost seventy Napoleons and hundreds of Hitlers. (I knew I was special.) There are, somewhat surprisingly, thirty-seven Stephen Colberts, and strangely, they're almost all in some way institutionalized. Quite an unusual coincidence, wouldn't you say?"

"Maybe," I responded, "but is there anybody in your survey that is unique?"

"Only one person has that distinction, and he is the subject of exhaustive scrutiny by associates of mine; a creature called Rush Limbaugh. There is some speculation that he may not in fact be a member of your race."

"You mean white or Anglo?" I goggled.

"No; human," he said without a trace of humor.

Okay, summon the elevator, the room is spinning. Mr. Nachron noted my expression of disbelief and chose to comfort me with these words.

"My boy, you didn't really think that I was entirely human, did you? This shouldn't be more surprising than black holes or antimatter. Much of what seems most challenging to the primitive mind is just beyond the horizon of man's knowledge and experience."

If this were a Vegas routine, I would be anxious for a good illusion, but I was reluctant to speculate where all this might be going. It didn't take much longer to find out as my host continued.

"What if," he said, "I could arrange a little traveling for you that may help to reunite you with the lovely Lynn, about whom you spoke so admiringly earlier this evening?"

Could he have heard that?

During the long silence that followed this question, I focused on a growing doubt about my new friend's sanity. Did he really say he and Rush weren't human? If not human, then what? He was unquestionably probing the contents of my addled mind, because his next remark was intended to address exactly that point.

"If it makes it easier, imagine billions of worlds populated by creatures to some degree analogous to humanity. They come into being, they reproduce, and some of them eventually perish. Then open your mind to the possible existence of beings outside that limited category. For our purposes, it might be convenient to picture angels and demons, only without the excess baggage of divinity, evil or wings."

Well that explains everything, I thought, now where's that elevator? Crystal has mace in her purse and can take care of herself.

"Give me just a moment more of your valuable time," he suggested, "and I'll tell you about an idea that may be of mutual benefit." He paused to be sure I had stopped moving toward the door. "If you would procure a few items for me, I would gratefully give you $100,000 and try to arrange a reunion with your beloved Lynn. If you prefer Euros, Swiss Francs or even platinum, it would be my pleasure to accommodate you."

He talked like I had already signed off on this unlikely proposal, and I had wryly assumed he was seeking unicorns or virgins. Even in the unlikely event I could capture things like that, how could he possibly reciprocate by producing the angel whose image dominated my dreams, when I had spent lots of time and money trying to do just that? What was I thinking? This is all bullcrap.

"Well, give it some thought," he went on, "and if you would go into the vestibule and pick up the packet on the Chinese table, you may keep it as a token of my gratitude for your conversation and companionship."

As I crossed into the small room, I relaxed at the prospect of my approaching departure and the relief it would bring. I'll just grab the item on the table, wake Crystal, and flee into the ordinary South Florida night.

I had barely touched Nachron's little gift, which turned out to be a silver coin wrapped in a page torn from a book, when I became suddenly aware of the light in the room brightening then darkening. A Doppler rumble that might herald an earthquake, and what seemed like a gravitational distortion that made me lightheaded but heavy-footed, stunned me into paralysis. As the rumble grew in intensity, the sound and light enfolded me and apparently robbed me of my awareness, since of this event I have no other memory.

"Time is the coin of your life. It is the only coin you have, and only you can determine how it will be spent. Be careful lest you let other people spend it for you."
Carl Sandburg

FIVE

Panama

I gradually awoke by battling layers of dizziness. The unrealistic dream I thought I was coming out of included the uncomfortable sensation of sand in my mouth and eyes and the warmth of the sun on most of my body. After cautiously removing what I could of the debris in my eye sockets, I strained through the brilliance of the sunlight to identify the single object casting an irregular shadow over me. What finally came into focus was the silhouette of a smallish long-haired person who had perhaps deliberately chosen a position to block my face from the sun. I closed my eyes again, hoping that the next time I opened them there would be something familiar in my field of vision that I could relate to.

When I eventually made the commitment to deal with these strange circumstances, she was still sitting there. I was lying on a deserted beach with a pretty young girl who sat with her arms around her legs and her cheek nearly touching her knees. She seemed to be as curious about me as I was her, but every time I looked directly into her eyes, she modestly looked downward to discourage my boldness. She wasn't just pretty. She was dark and windblown and mesmerizing, and if I hadn't been so confused about how we came to be here, I would have felt pretty good about sharing this beach with her. I thought I could tempt her into conversation by using my gentlest tone and making no sudden movements, but she didn't seem to speak English so I said "Espanol?" There was a tiny hint of a smile and a nearly imperceptible nod that told me I might reach her with my unpolished Spanish. She patiently listened to me struggling to form sentences as I slowly pried my exhausted body from the sand. When I stood up and began brushing myself off, she rose and smoothed her plain white dress so it wouldn't be caught by a wind that might expose her knees.

Of all the questions I could think of to ask her, the only one she responded to was to share her name, Marta, in a voice so timid I could barely hear it over the coastal breeze. In her world, as I was later to learn, making new friends carried unusual significance, but at that moment I was still trying to solve my own mysteries. I was alert enough to know I wasn't dreaming, but where was I? Did I drink so much that I stumbled onto a movie set? Was I drugged and sent on a surprise vacation by playful friends? I wasn't even close to connecting this apparently friendly environment with any memory, but circumstances would eventually help me suspend my sense of disbelief.

    I walked to the water's edge with the hope of seeing coastal Fort Lauderdale or at least the highrises of Miami to the south, but the beach curved sharply in both directions so I knew it wasn't Florida. I've been on every Atlantic Beach between Key West and Vero, and this spot wasn't part of that coastline. Also, the water was too cold and the trees were all wrong. I must have been muttering to myself as I retraced my steps back to Marta because she looked at me strangely, probably wondering why the tide had dropped me on her shore that day.

    Some time later, as the sun neared the horizon, she turned and slowly began to walk away from the sea, looking frequently behind her as if to encourage me to accompany her. This wasn't exactly accurate since if I approached her too closely as we walked, she would deliberately accelerate in order to preserve the distance between us. Being the rear guard wasn't totally without its advantages. It gave me more time to reflect on my personal dilemma while offering the superb view of Marta gracefully choosing her steps ahead of me. Once animated by motion, she elevated herself beyond simple beauty. Why I started thinking about Lynn at that moment I couldn't say for sure, but I had trouble allowing a competing vision, no matter how appealing, to intrude on my memory of her.

    I had to suppress this strange mental conflict in order to cope with my new surroundings.

Speaking my pidgin Spanish on what appeared to be a tropical Pacific beach seemed like an impossibility, but until I could extricate myself, I intended to deal with obstacles patiently and thoughtfully. The only useful fragment of memory that I was able to salvage was of an odd little bald man who offered an improbable reward if I would agree to perform some vague service, so I fell in behind my guide while my mind wondered.

Marta's confidence as she picked her way barefoot through the green tangle reassured me that I didn't have to worry about spiders and snakes, but I hoped we would come upon a village or at least a tree house where someone else could explain things to me. After ten minutes of winding our way through the foliage, we came to a cleared area of neat, well-maintained wooden structures. The majority of these were small enough to be residential, but there were also two slightly larger official looking buildings. I stopped long enough in front of the largest one to read the sign on the façade, which was barely within the scope of my linguistic skills. I might have had a little trouble translating it word-for-word, but the gist of the message informed me that I was standing in front of the administrative headquarters of a Lazareto in Panama.

I finally had some useful information. Aside from my beautiful new friend, I could occupy myself with three thoughts:

1) Panama?
2) Does the word Lazareto mean I'm in a Leper Colony?

3) Isolating victims of leprosy (Hansen's disease now) in remote colonies was discontinued decades ago, wasn't it?

    My head throbbed with the growing fear that the fantastic nature of my situation was solidifying into an uncomfortable reality. All of the elements of the experience and knowledge that anchored my existence became a kind of fiction that clearly did not apply here. I believe in certainty, and I was shocked to learn that in my case, certainty was merely a set of invalid assumptions. My new reality consisted of a mysterious girl in a time and place that was utterly strange to me, with a single exception. There was in my buttoned pants pocket, a large Panamanian silver coin dated 1904, which I vaguely remembered acquiring some indeterminate amount of time ago. The coin was wrapped in a page torn from an old catalogue with the illustration of another coin and some information regarding its mintage and rarity. Finally, in neat handwriting in the margin were the words "Trade this for a choice new colony coin."

Palo Seco Leper Colony, 1916

Photo from National Archives

"Time is a great teacher, but unfortunately it kills its pupils." Louis Hector Berlioz

SIX

Palo Seco

By now, I should have made a connection between Mr. Nachron's odd proposal, the sounds, the noise, and my arrival on a beach from the past, but I was stubborn and skeptical, thus realization came a bit slowly. I have spent much of my life blundering into unfamiliar situations, but in this instance I dawdled for a bit to consider my options. It was dawning on me that I was presumably a healthy visitor to a very unusual and specialized location that existed decades before my birth. Most people would feel entitled to a decent amount of time to wallow in hesitancy and disbelief, but I had already begun making the mental adjustments that would enable me to adapt. I freely confess to an infatuation with beautiful tropical settings, mysterious attractive women and challenges, and here were all three. From a distance of roughly twenty yards, I could see Marta, not impatient, not beckoning, just staring in my direction. My romance with her had begun at that moment.

During the first quarter of the twentieth century, lepers and their families all over the world lived relatively long and normal lives in their isolated communities. Although those obviously afflicted with Hansen's disease were discouraged from interacting with healthy populations, they were not spared from pain, violence, greed and the other weaknesses that man is heir to. As in the outside world, there were marriages and other celebrations to help distract them from the monotony of simple survival. The shock of how I came to be among them would no doubt wane as I prepared to confront whatever fate had in store for me in Palo Seco. The fantastic transition I had made in no way altered the normal human need for sustenance and companionship, and Marta had made such a hypnotic impact on me that the most troubling aspects of my new life began to seem surmountable.

Her home was half of a small wooden structure that served as a storeroom, with a tiny, meagerly furnished living area. Since she lived in a community where cleanliness was highly regarded, her cubicle was immaculate and her pitifully small stack of clothing and towels was freshly laundered.

The first night I spent in Panama, I slept with one of her towels around my shoulders curled up near her door like an animal that knows where breakfast might come from. My exhaustion must have required a long rest, since when I stiffly awoke, Marta was again looking at me, this time not without some comfortable familiarity. She showed me where to bathe after she introduced me to one of the administrators, who generously furnished me with a fresh shirt and a bar of harsh soap.

I was in fairly good spirits in spite of the circumstances, and I was happy to answer the many questions that were put to me later that day by Marta and a few others. Of course I could hardly tell what I thought was the truth, so I constructed what I hoped was a believable story about my accent and my strange appearance among them.

I carefully explained how I'd fallen off a fishing boat that had strayed close to shore, but the peculiar looks I received from those most curious about the circumstances of my arrival told me I was missing something. It seems that the winds and seas had been unseasonably calm for the seventy-two hours prior to my arrival, so falling off a slow-moving boat without other crew members noticing and rescuing me seemed doubtful. I regained their confidence by explaining that the skipper and many of the crew were under the constant influence of alcohol. There was a cultural awareness of the damaging influence of rum on the well-being of any community, but recently, a violent incident in the colony was thought to be the direct result of abuse of some intoxicant. I emphasized my good luck at being found by Marta and answered a few incidental questions gratefully and submissively, so it seemed I had nearly won their trust. I have always been able to treat the truth as a kind of hypothetical gel that may be molded into a serviceable form, and as no one could recall any person sneaking into a leper colony to do mischief, my hosts had no further reason to be wary.

Although Marta was the particular object of my curiosity and attention, many of her other neighbors, including healthy volunteers, were kind and accommodating. I was as a satyr among hyperions, but I believed that lengthy exposure to people with such a richness of spirit might eventually make me more deserving of their companionship. To that end, I was especially available to Marta, and my vulnerability must have been appealing to her since she demonstrated her gratitude for my helpfulness by rewarding me with her beautiful and innocent smile. I started to believe that I could be happy indefinitely as her friend and guardian, although my baser nature would occasionally produce a pang of desire that embarrassed me.

I endured the passage of the next forty-eight hours coming to terms with the growing belief that Palo Seco was to be my new home. The hottest part of each day found me walking on the beach watching birds dive and clouds race across the horizon, as if the elegant reality that nature provided might distract me from the fading grasp of who I had once been.

The time I spent in the company of others was chiefly dedicated to familiarizing myself with the habits and rhythm of life in the colony, while never really letting Marta out of my sight. In the afternoon of my third day in Panama, two of the younger children had tempted her into chasing them around the common area and their happy laughter made passers-by stop and smile. I could only wonder what her childhood could've been like. Was she misdiagnosed at a young age and torn from her parents side or was she banished from the company of so-called healthy people later in life? Was there a husband or children somewhere? She wasn't old enough to have had too lengthy a past, but it seemed likely to have been full of pain I could hardly hope to comprehend.

There was one positive consequence of submitting to the strangeness of a new reality. Thoughts of Lynn, which popped into my mind with the same frequency as ever, were not sufficiently vivid to produce the pain and loneliness I had gotten used to. I hadn't given up my obsessive desire for her, but I had lost enough of the emotional fragility that accompanied my memories to appreciate the most important component of this new setting.

For the most part, I learned to amble around like a neutered cat, deciding alternately between enjoying the shade of a tree or flopping down in a sunbeam with my eyes half-closed. The sight of Marta carrying water or helping someone else with a chore however, would cause me to hop immediately to her side and offer my services, which she learned to accept graciously. I had a series of very realistic dreams a few years ago in which I was the favorite counselor to a Czarina, and even though I couldn't understand a word she said, I was able to sense her wishes and act upon them successfully.

Marta was well on the way to becoming my Czarina until the night she surprised me by inviting me into her room. Before that moment, for obvious reasons, we hadn't come within two feet of each other, and I was uncomfortable with the awkwardness which was certain to follow. She asked me to sit opposite her on a woven mat, and she taught me more about physical love in the next three hours than I ever expect to learn elsewhere. My previous experience with lovemaking now seems clumsy and bestial by comparison, and the feebly subdued hunger I always attached to sexuality was abandoned in favor of Marta's whispered instructions.

"Do not move quickly or say anything. I will tell you what I want."

She ordered me to close my eyes so that only the flickering of the single candle could be seen through the thinness of my eyelids. She told me to lift my hand in front of me with palm extended and be very calm and patient. When she suggested that I open my eyes, I was stunned to see that she had silently removed her dress and placed herself before me with her palm near mine and a modest smile of such beauty that I ached not only with desire, but awe at being allowed to witness this compelling sight. Her lips were full and beads of moisture were forming around her mouth and on her forehead. Her breasts were small and perfect, rhythmically moving in a reflection of the tempo of her heart and quickening breath. She then told me to close my eyes once more and be very still, as it was her intention to come closer.

Her scent came to me as the distance between us closed. It was the intoxicating combination of young fresh moist skin and something vaguely floral, probably a resource of local origin. I sensed her then on the palm of my still extended hand as the warmth of hers perceptibly influenced my newly enhanced awareness. For me to feel that extraordinary sensation, we could only have been millimeters apart, and that tiny thermal increment produced a disproportionate flush and swelling in the rest of my body. We remained so long in stillness that I thought there might be a real possibility of fainting.

If that were the entirety of the programme, I would not have had energy to cheer for an encore, but she had just begun. In the next hours, she positioned herself so that all exposed (I was still in shorts) parts of my torso were treated to proximity to some radiating appendage of hers. I concentrated on the illusion of opening every pore on my body to receive what she offered and when it finally ended, I was in tears from the effort and the release from it. When I opened my eyes she was lying a few feet away, a sight I shall remember beyond the grave.

When you believe you are suffering from an incurable communicable disease, which Marta did although she had no visible lesions, the human touch must be considered from an entirely different perspective. Her versatile imagination had replaced physical contact with something almost equally combustible, and I believe I was the subject of her first experiment. Plenty of females would laughingly assume that it was egotistical of me to claim first privilege, but I had fallen completely under her influence, and quite naturally, I refused to acknowledge the possibility that I might not be her first or last.

I had already started mentally adjusting to what I believed would be my future at Marta's side, and the pleasure we might both take when she learned I did not fear her touch. I was happily reviewing the order in which I would soon introduce her body to my caresses as I walked to the administration building the next morning, where I had decided to unravel the mystery of the numismatic contents of my pocket. By this simple act, I would disconnect myself from the last tangible vestige of my past.

On arriving at the offices of the Palo Seco Colonial Authority, I learned that word of my abrupt appearance had already spread through the population. I was welcomed with grace and hospitality by a kindly white-haired physician named Antonio Lopez, who showed me to a chair in his small office and asked me how he could be of service. I thanked him for seeing me without notice and reached into my pocket to remove the coin for him to examine.

Since almost every civilized country of that period produced coins of similar size and silver purity, he recognized my 1904 fifty centesimos as having value equivalent to a U.S. silver dollar of the same era. He also noticed the image of a coin on the page before him, and since he had recently received a shipment of these specially produced items, he was more than a little surprised that they would already be illustrated in an English language catalogue complete with mintage figures. As he patiently explained, there was a general fear that coins handled by lepers might carry the infectious agent to healthy hands, so the need for a medium of exchange exclusively for the use of isolated populations was acted upon by the Panamanian government. The result was the manufacture of a small number of coins in six denominations, all undated but possibly produced around 1919, to satisfy the various needs of the colony.

Dr. Lopez then opened his desk drawer to show me a number of shiny coins with rectangular holes in the center that had yet to see circulation. In response, I acted on a vague memory from another time, offering to trade him my silver coin in exchange for one of his little brass ones. After briefly explaining what a bad deal I was making, he gave me two coins for mine and our business was concluded. Since shaking hands was a somewhat uncommon practice under these presumably threatening circumstances, we salaamed and I took my leave.

For whatever vague purpose I had just consummated a supposedly one-sided transaction I was uncertain, but I enjoyed a peculiar sense of satisfaction at having completed an assignment. As I walked across the common area, the sun suddenly seemed too bright, and I couldn't imagine the source of that approaching roar, although it seemed familiar. I knew I was losing consciousness, and if that were not alarming enough, I was most stricken by the terrible certainty that I would never see Marta again.

Mike Corbett

SEVEN

"Ronny my friend, are you refreshed? You've been sleeping for hours."

I opened my eyes to the jolly round face of Mr. Nachron, who offered coffee, tea, breakfast and lots of questions about my well-being. "Mr. Nachron, I must have passed out. Did I seem ill?" I asked.

"Nonsense, my boy, and please call me Albert. You're quite well." He was positively effervescent. "Did you enjoy your little adventure?"

I felt uncertain about sharing the particulars of what must have been a very vivid dream with this amiable elf, so I admitted to a little confusion.

"Check your pocket," he instructed, "and I'll help you clear away some of the cobwebs."

As I reached into the pocket where my hand closed around the two small coins, I became suddenly aware that dreaming and illness were imaginary, and the coins with the fragmentary memories of how I happened to possess them were reality.

"May I see what you retrieved?" he asked as I slowly produced the tattered page with the coins inside. "My goodness, there are two! Well, no harm done. I can send one with you on your next errand."

The combination of fatigue, anger, disbelief and apprehension caused me to react by sputtering frantically for a few moments and then fainting. I dreamed about trotting around in hell with a crossbow, selecting a demon with eight point antlers and escaping with my trophy before the other residents had time to object. The words "next errand" were reverberating through my brain as I once again regained consciousness. I summoned the energy to croak a miserably defiant "What do you mean, errand?" to the sympathetic face of Mr. Nachron, "and where's Crystal?"

He assured me that Crystal was sent home safely in a taxi after being told that I left to do a small favor for him. Then he smiled and patiently recounted what had happened to me, beginning with a reiteration of the previous night's conversation, a brief elaboration of the scientific mumbo-jumbo that explained my ability to travel back into the previous century, and concluding with his pleasure at being the new owner of the two small coins. He assured me that they would now be unquestionably the two finest examples of that rare series extant, although he would only need one for his collection, so the other could be disposed of. It ended up in a Civil War era vessel doing service as a gasket, but I'm getting ahead of myself.

The evolution of my disbelief into simple skepticism and then to credulity did not come immediately. I had come to terms with the narrowness and inaccuracy of many of my observations, and I slowly learned to sacrifice them in the face of mounting contradictory evidence. The whole thing was pretty hard to swallow however, and if I agreed to any more of Nachron's requests, it was clear that I would have to place a lot of trust in people and ideas that were alien to me.

In the next few hours, I was able to pull myself from the comfortable couch, eat breakfast, and gather my thoughts while showering. My obliging host followed me around with profuse apologies about tricking me into a trip to Panama and a wheedling presentation intended to help me make up my mind about the collaboration he hoped for. Along with the many enticements he proposed was the attractive offer of residence of indefinite length at an apartment that was way too large for one small person. I would not have been too surprised if he somehow knew that I had recently been asked to give up my own modest dwelling, which stood in the way of downtown development.

Timing is the crucial element in the decision making process, and I was being made increasingly aware of the advantages that Nachron's proposals offered. The vacuum of my life due to Lynn's absence, the need for some extraordinary stimuli to justify my existence, and the chance to avoid homelessness, all argued for my consent to do his bidding; so I was in.

I spent a couple of recuperative days enjoying the warm water and sunsets of Fort Lauderdale beach and pronounced myself fit for another mission during the evening of the third day.

"Excellent my boy," he responded. "I will give you a brief preparation and you could be on your way very soon."

That preparation consisted of about an hour of general information about the months before the end of World War II. His patriotic slant was intended to rub off on me, I assumed, but I was becoming uncomfortable at the prospect of going somewhere that people were shooting at each other.

"Don't concern yourself about that," he chuckled. "You will be going only as far as New Mexico, and you may expect only civil treatment from its peaceful inhabitants."

I had hoped for a decent amount of time for reflection, but Nachron was not one to waste time once the course was set. The noise began, as before, and my empty stomach lurched as I was propelled to my destination.

"Our battered suitcases were piled on the sidewalk again; we had longer ways to go. But no matter, the road is life."
                                           Jack Kerouac

EIGHT

New Mexico

Hitchhiking has been a sensibly economical, if somewhat haphazard, means of travel for centuries. If you wanted to go someplace, you simply planted yourself beside some thoroughfare with the hope of inspiring charitable impulses in passers-by. By the end of the twentieth century however, the obvious romantic appeal of sharing a ride with a stranger had nearly vanished.

Before I was mature enough to fear earthquakes or air pollution, I spent a few summers in Southern California, where the cultural ethos of that environment lent itself to generous gestures. I rarely spent more than a minute or two on the coastal highway before some stoner or soccer mom picked me up, surfboard and all. It was a mixed blessing that I was long and wiry with shoulder-length white sun-bleached hair, blue eyes and an honest face, since shirtless surfers were the occasional targets of the impure appetites of stoners and soccer moms. I squirmed out of a slow-moving car once in such a panic that I left my board behind.

The twenty-first century adaptation of this venerable system of conveyance is so rife with predatory behaviors that nobody really knows which is more dangerous, hitching a ride or picking somebody up. Violent pedophiles have spoiled it for the rest of us.

Luckily (so far anyway), I found myself in the Southwestern United States in the 1940's and hitchhiking was at its zenith. Cars were expensive, fuel was rationed, and the allies were acting in concert to preserve life, liberty, and the pursuit of happiness. This cooperative energy made sharing a ride almost patriotic, so I felt quite at ease with my latest assignment. I had merely to wait for a particular car and induce the driver, of whom I knew nothing, to bring me to a gas station where I was to obtain a very valuable but ordinary looking scrap of paper, then wait for Nachron to spirit me away. This sounded like child's play compared to my prior adventure, so I anticipated my immediate future with no particular trepidation.

The temperature had fallen a few degrees since midafternoon, but the wind was light as the clouds on the western horizon turned slightly red across the biggest sky I had ever seen. I expelled a fresh lungful of desert air and considered my fortune with anticipatory optimism and the absence of obligations like a 9 to 5 job or alimony. Once in the designated car, I was told that I had simply to lift the mat on the floor of the trunk where I would find that small piece of paper.

    I knew I wasn't too far from Santa Fe or Albuquerque, so I hoped I might even have time for a taste of Southwestern cuisine. After my previous trip, I could foresee no similar obstacles, so I scanned the distant horizon for the car Nachron described and made myself comfortable squatting on the still sun-warmed sand at the side of the road. I had been prepared to remain alert for the arrival of a nondescript American built sedan with a dent on the front quarter panel that could be spotted at some distance, but it wasn't exactly rush hour, so I timed the intervals between cars passing in either direction. The average exceeded ten minutes, but I never felt more alive, so boredom was not an issue.

    Before the sun got too low in the sky, I saw the vehicle I was waiting for. The car was exactly as described, with a pair of average looking guys in the front who amiably waved me into the back seat when they saw I was heading in the same direction they were. I introduced myself and shook hands with each of them once we were under way, and was surprised to learn that my chauffeur was none other than Richard Feynman, the famous physicist. The other guy, whose name escapes me, had been picked up a few miles back and seemed also to have some business in Santa Fe. It turns out that Dr. Feynman, whose stellar reputation as a theoretician may outlive even Nachron, had borrowed a car from a friend of his at Los Alamos to visit his critically ill wife in Albuquerque. Los Alamos, you may recall, was the location in which the United States government had secretly assembled the brilliant minds responsible for the construction and test of a nuclear weapon.

The Manhattan Project was Oppenheimer, Bethe, Feynman and a host of other scientists and engineers whose ingenuity, for better or worse, changed the world. It was very tempting to mention some of the remarkable advances science had made by the twenty-first century, but that may have distracted Dr. Feynman and confused me, so we talked about art, music, and playfully, the cube root of 1729.03, which I knew how to approximate from reading one of his books. He would have been fascinated by the process by which I was able to read a book before he wrote it, but even for a character with an imagination as nimble as his, my story might have been a bit overwhelming. He liked to talk, and anyone lucky enough to hear him could benefit from his insights,[*] so I sprawled out in the back seat and wished the trip would take longer.

I closed my eyes and considered once again the bright light and loud noise that meant I was crossing into another era. The exceptional man driving the car was a few weeks away from witnessing the light and noise emitted by the first test of a nuclear weapon, and thus another era, so we had something in common. In fact, he may have been the only man to actually see the thing go off without the dark glasses that were passed out to shield the eyes of the observers from ultraviolet rays caused by the explosion, since he knew that a simple truck windshield would be ample protection.

---

[*] Bohr and Einstein occasionally dropped in on his lectures

If all those brilliant men could have known where this was headed, would the world be different now?

I must have eventually fallen asleep, but I gradually awakened to a change in the engine's pitch and a flapping sound as we limped into Santa Fe with a rapidly flattening tire. My new friend on the passenger side of the front seat woke up just in time to volunteer us for the chore of changing it, a duty that had to be performed again a short time later outside of the city. This was the end of the line for me, however, since we pulled into the gas station that would be my last stop. While fumbling with the spare tire, I had discovered that unimportant looking piece of paper with some vague symbols and a bit of math on it, and buried it deep in my pocket. I was reasonably sure that I had not been seen removing the item Nachron wanted from the trunk, but I raised my head nonchalantly to see if there were any curious onlookers. I saw nothing suspicious to pique my awareness so I relaxed my guard. When the tire (another war time shortage) was removed and eventually replaced, I wished my companions a safe trip, thanked Dr. Feynman for his kindness, and looked around for an authentic Southwestern meal. I even considered ordering takeout if my time was as limited as I thought.

There was a tiny restaurant connected to the station with a few feet of counter space of dubious cleanliness, but the smell of cornmeal and beans was tantalizing. Before I had time to give the only visible employee my order, I was joined by two serious looking individuals who flanked me ominously. These fellows, it turned out, were associates of the gentleman who owned the car Feynman had borrowed to go to his wife's side.

Klaus Fuchs, who worked on the Project, had been informed about the critically ill Mrs. Feynman so he volunteered his car when it was needed. Mr. Fuchs, as I was later to learn, was a spy whose obvious intention was to share information generated at Los Alamos with the Germans. If I had known that, I might have guessed that my dinner companions were Nazis, but I had not planned to be confronted by antagonists, so I just pretended not to notice them and kept to myself. Before I could finish my meal, I felt an urging pressure on my arms to rise and accompany the two very fit looking gentlemen outside.

    Mysterious codes and thugs aren't so common in espionage movies anymore, so I could be forgiven for my naiveté. Nowadays its possible for a person with a telescope and a good camera to capture images from a laptop reflected off the eyeballs of its user, so violence is less useful in this evolved new world of intelligence gathering.

    Remember, I still didn't know for sure who these guys were, but I limply allowed myself to be led outside as I measured the exact distance and location of throat and kneecap. When you cannot possibly avoid fighting two people, you have to have a very good plan, and engaging two opponents simultaneously, or going after the bigger one first are bad strategies.[*] The best hope to prevail in such a situation is to immediately disable the least formidable adversary if possible, so you can give full attention to the other without the distraction of

---

[*] This plan generally includes physical confrontations with a man and a woman, a woman and a dog, etc.

being attacked from behind. I had just chosen the object of my first assault, when the noise and light produced the confusion that paralyzed all of us.

Mike Corbett

NINE

"Well, my boy, may I presume these gentlemen are friends of yours?"

The words he spoke were puzzling since I was still a bit confused by my trip across more than sixty years. As my vision and judgment returned to relative clarity, I looked around and saw my two would-be captors on the floor beside me, as addled as I was after Panama, with the mini-sorcerer clucking disapprovingly at the unexpected arrival of Nazis in Fort Lauderdale. I could hardly claim any credit for an unwanted intrusion since Nachron was responsible for orchestrating this adventure, and if I could have chosen, I would have at least come back with girl Nazis. I assumed that a snap of fingers or a wave of wand would propel these Teutonic roughnecks back to the crumbling Reich, but apparently it was not so simple.

Nachron patiently explained that dragging people into the future and then sending them back to the past was more complex and troublesome than doing it in the reverse order. While he articulated the various considerations, my mind was wandering into the vengeful plans I might contrive to solve our problem while tossing in a bit of righteous irony. Not necessarily in the order of my personal preference, these notions came to me:

1) Put them on a flight to Tel Aviv with written plans to blow up the Knesset.
2) Circumcise them, and then send them back to the Lodz ghetto.
3) Confine them in a Dresden jail the day before the firebombs were delivered, to acquire more incendiary information.

I was disturbed from my contemplations by the unmistakably clipped syllables of German, spoken with as much authority as Nachron required in order to compel our guests to snap to attention. Helmut and Hans, as I was to learn, were responding to a verbal code that announced the presence of a superior, and were instructed to sit quietly on the couch. Nachron drew me aside to share his concerns with me, sotto voce, since these Nazis were obviously fluent enough in English to help steal secrets in America.

"The problem my boy," he confided, "is how to deal fairly with your two playmates. I am neither inclined nor obliged to administer justice, so I must deliver them back to their own time; but wherever I choose to send them, they are destined to face dire consequences."

I could see nothing objectionable about that, but apparently Nachron had a sentimental side, since he proposed a bizarre compromise.

He thought it would be nice if before their grim return to firebombs or war trials, they might like a bit of a romp in Fort Lauderdale. He implied that I squire them around to outdoor concerts and beach volleyball games so they might experience the world with its post-Nazi refinements. Helmut and Hans were, after all, just a couple of somewhat brainwashed German twenty-somethings who knew only jackboots and propaganda, so who was I to deny them a taste of South Florida hospitality?

I would not typically object to a weekend of stone crabs and lap dances, but could I depend on the boys from the bund to behave rationally in the modern equivalent of Sodom and Gomorrah? How would a couple of guys who think partying is a glass of Schnapps and the singing of patriotic songs deal with a multi-ethnic society where whites, blacks, accountants and clergymen regularly take ecstasy and send text messages from their vehicles while speeding to strip clubs?

Considering my immediate past, you might assume I would be reluctant to undertake this new challenge, but I was already looking up the number of the limousine service. If I could keep them off the crack pipe and away from the transvestite hookers, Hans and Helmut might take a few good memories back to the fatherland.

In the next few days we didn't visit a single museum or library. We did manage brief tours of Broward General Hospital, Broward and Dade County jails, the German Consulate, and inadvertently, an after hours club for transgender folks. Hans even met a Jewish girl who could deftly remove the pimento from an olive and return it to her martini using only her tongue, but she was married to a rich orthodontist, so her future availability would have been a problem even if Hans could have stayed.

    Helmut found a way to disappear for twelve hours on an airboat he borrowed to impress a stripper, but with the help of the Seminole Nation and a rented helicopter with pilot paid for by Nachron, we were able to retrieve them before they succumbed to insect bites. The Indians who aided in the rescue made a tasteless joke about the ability of a python to consume an entire stripper or vice versa, but my charges didn't get it, so I cast my eyes downward as I grinned.

    If Nachron had known that he was not underwriting poetry readings and visits to orphanages, he might have balked at the expense, but I could not be relied upon to organize and provide such civilized recreations. Given a choice between an eternity to be spent in heaven or Las Vegas, I bet Hans, Helmut, and half of the rest of us would take a bad lounge act over centuries of harp music. My instructions were to use my best judgment in planning our diversions, but since I rarely permit judgment to inhibit impulse, the three of us ended up in a foul-smelling heap on Nachron's carpet five days later. Our host scowled and paced for a while, snapped out a German phrase that made my companions blush, and then asked if I would make a pot of coffee. When I returned from the kitchen, I saw we would need only two cups.

    I went to my room early that night but there was too much on my mind to properly relax. Mr. Nachron had never made it clear whether I was playing a role and thus altering our history, or simply acting out one of an infinite number of permutations that might be part of multi-dimensional histories. I went into the kitchen with the hope that a snack might distract and liberate me from issues I couldn't possibly understand, and was surprised to find Nachron with a pile of old documents in front of him. Did he ever sleep?

"Mr. Nachron, could I rest more comfortably if I could be certain that the net effect of all my activities was positive?"

He put down what I later learned was a hand written papal decree, very old and very rare, to respond.

"For the sake of simplicity my friend, you may assume that the whole of existence is a zero-sum game. If there are small disparities in the balance of forces in one dimension, they are counter-balanced by similar but opposite variations in another. Observable nature demands eventual stability from positive and negative charges, matter and antimatter, and a host of other analogous examples. The universe, with minor and temporary exceptions, functions admirably thus. In your specific case, the relative impact of a success or a failure is inconsequential since any turbulence you are responsible for will prompt a compensatory response. The unexpected intrusion of Helmut and Hans for example, was an inconvenience to both of us, but their destiny was ultimately to fail. We merely protracted their failure. In actuality, if our interference had somehow contaminated that failure, there were other Nazis waiting on the sidelines to produce the necessarily negative outcome." He paused long enough to go to another room and retrieve a pile of papers which he suggested that I read at my leisure.

Helmut and Hans weren't really incompetent, but they were unlucky for many reasons. My intrusion into their mission would have been bad enough, but to be accidentally vacuumed up by Nachron; that was a real long shot. The two guys my host wanted me to read about, William Colepaugh and Erick Gimpel, were also sent to the United States to get information about the Manhattan Project. They crossed the Atlantic in a U-boat and then came by raft to a shoreline near Bar Harbor Maine in the winter of 1944. Due to a general lack of preparation, the infiltration had virtually no chance of success, but the two spies were able to blend in for a time in the northeastern United States without raising any alarms.

Colepaugh, a disaffected American citizen ultimately lost his feelings of commitment to the Third Reich and confessed his crime, naming Gimpel during the process. As Nachron had implied, these two guys were likely to produce a decent failure if their predecessors were unequal to the task. My research also yielded the interesting information that Helmut and Hans weren't the last Nazis to vacation in Florida. Colepaugh, after serving seventeen years in prison, ended up in a convalescent home in Florida where he may survive today.

TEN

Crystal's Adventure

I was more fatigued by my adolescent fling with the Nazis than I cared to admit. I intended to spend the next few days recuperating, but circumstances beyond my control interrupted the scholarly interlude that my host had generously provided. I never would have believed that hand-drawn maps of the Holy Roman Empire could be so interesting, but Albert Nachron was enthusiastically making a case for not only their historical importance, but for the craftsmanship required to create them. Just as I was starting to believe that discussions like this could be as much fun as tennis or a walk to the beach, there was an aggressively loud knock at the door that surprised even Nachron.

When I opened it, Crystal brushed by me and nearly bowled over our host, kicking her shoes off and flopping onto the couch in a single motion.

"Okay," she said, "I've got thirty-six consecutive hours before my next shift and I expect to be entertained. If you two chumps aren't up to the job, I'm going to rent a Harley and drive to Naples."

It was unlikely that Crystal, the Harley, or Naples would survive that plan, so we agreed to her terms.

"First," I asked. "How did you get past the attendant? Isn't he supposed to call and announce visitors before sending guests up?"

"Well," she purred, "I've never had to pay a cover charge or wait behind a velvet rope before. Why should this guy be any different from the rest of you?"

Albert seemed confused about this most natural human weakness, but looking at Crystal with one beautiful leg thrown over the top cushion of the couch, and her arms bare to the shoulder and reaching over her head to stretch like a feral cat, made me sympathize with the attendant's failure to discharge his duties.

The plan we eventually acted on was to take the water taxi as far as the Intracoastal Waterway, have a light lunch on the beach before a walk to the port, then return to the apartment early enough to have cocktails at sunset before deciding where to have dinner. Fort Lauderdale is beautiful when the sun is low in the sky. The flora, the ocean and the old Florida architecture on the east side reflect the failing light in a sensuous display that makes Canadian couples fall in love here.

After Nachron and I cleaned up, we talked while Crystal showered and dressed in the guest bedroom. In surprisingly short order she emerged, hair barely towel dried, no makeup (she didn't need it), and in the de rigeur Fort Lauderdale uniform, shorts and tee shirt. Her flip-flops were slightly larger than her newly pedicured feet might require, but any St. Tropez teenager will tell you that the best way to make feet appear small and well-shaped is to keep the toes well within the sandal.

We drove north to the Fort Lauderdale Tennis Club to watch a couple of talented Russian teenagers play a set in the shadow of the clubhouse while we drank mojitos and sampled a plate of tapas. Nachron, in the quietest minutes I had ever seen him, was hypnotized by the effect topspin was having on the trajectory of the ball during the long rallies. Without considering the sophistication of his audience, he started babbling about gravity and angular momentum, so Crystal immediately brought him a third mojito.

In order not to imperil our travel back and forth across town, I had only one drink, and seeing that some of the elderly husbands were paying too close attention to Crystal's legs under their wives' disapproving glares, we chose to leave. I unlocked and opened the passenger door for my friends while Nachron stopped to show Crystal something interesting in the darkening sky. If any of us were paying attention, there was also something interesting happening in the dark parking lot.

An iguana, probably drawn to the heat of the engine, had left his spot in the undercarriage of my two door Chevrolet to crawl under the front seat while we dithered. Iguanas are not native to South

Florida, but they seem happy here since their numbers have steadily grown enough to make people uncomfortable. Although they are not aggressive, they have a threatening appearance and will grow to a length of five feet or more including tail, biting only if threatened.

    I had driven about a mile toward everybody in Fort Lauderdale's favorite Greek restaurant near Oakland Park Boulevard on A-1-A, when I became aware of the uninvited passenger. His tail whipped out from directly between my legs and thrashed from side to side before I could even identify what kind of a threat we were dealing with. I veered to the side of the road so Crystal, who shared my surprise, and I could bale out. Albert, more or less unaware of the nature of the intruder and somewhat confined in the back seat, vaulted over the headrest and squirmed out the door as he caught sight of the beast. Crystal, in the meantime had found a stick which she extended asking "Which one of you girls will escort that thing out of the car so we can go eat?"

    It fell to me as the driver to be the iguana herder, so I poked at it a few times and it obligingly scuttled out the door. During the resumption of our drive, we speculated on how iguanas, pythons, or lionfish might have some medical benefit, and how quickly they could evolve from perceived pests to blessings. Nachron, in his knowing manner, winked, burped and made a remark about lionfish tasting like chicken, so he might have known something we didn't. All the old fishing boat captains remember the days when fish with too many bright colors were considered poisonous, so dolphin (mahi, not bottle-nosed mammals) were thrown back as so-called trash fish.

Driving east at thirty-five miles per hour, our musings were interrupted by the return of our unwanted guest. The iguana had miraculously appeared on the hood of the car, and like some kind of satanic hood ornament, he seemed to be finding that vantage point superior to the cranny beneath the car to which I had unwittingly shooed him. We pulled into the restaurant parking lot and once again coaxed the persistent amphibian to depart, this time watching to be sure he was well away from the car before we went inside. If the Greek restaurant's kitchen staff is as talented as I think, the menu may eventually feature an interesting new kabob.

At nine o'clock on a balmy night near the ocean, there's just no reason not to sit outside, so we ordered another round of cocktails and made ourselves comfortable. Since my two companions had drunk considerably more than I had, I wondered if I could cook up a little diversion that I had spent some time considering. Could Crystal do what I had done? If she could just enjoy a tiny sample of what I had experienced, could some of her confusion about exactly what was going on with Nachron and me be dispelled? I knew that she might need a little proof that I wasn't crazy, and if I could induce the slightly tipsy wizard beside me to give her a little demonstration, it would go a long way toward dissolving her skepticism.

To my surprise, neither Crystal nor Nachron thought it would be a big deal. For one thing, Crystal seemed unconvinced that the whole thing wasn't a trick. For Nachron's part, liquor intruded on his typically cautious attitude regarding his "gift". Before I had even concluded my explanatory pitch about the virtues of time travel, since for Crystal that was the simplest description, she started to blur, then fade. I gawked at Nachron, who seemed quite calm, and pointed at the not quite empty seat across from us.

"Wasn't this according to both of your wishes? I assumed we were all in agreement, but there is no need to be concerned. She will be rejoining us shortly."

ELEVEN

The Studio

Crystal, when she had regained her composure, was a little surprised that she found herself on a comfortable chair apparently sitting for a portrait.* It was a cloudless day and the many studio windows were open to admit light and a breeze which would not have chilled her if she had clothes on. Her first instinct was to grab the nearest piece of cloth that would partially cover her, and escape to the outside. But what if Nachron could really be capable of the miracles that were described to her and she was in a country that persecuted women for not wearing headwear? She could be stoned to death!

---

* Crystal shared a more detailed account with me months after it happened, and there is no reason to doubt her veracity.

Before doing anything hasty, she forced herself to consider the circumstances. It didn't seem like she was being held captive. Now that the dizziness she had initially felt had gone, she wasn't uncomfortable or hungry. The room was sparsely furnished but it had a great number of sketches and paintings in various stages of completion, and from what she could deduce, the content was neither lurid nor violent. She had begun to shed the nerves she had arrived with, so when she was joined by a smallish man with a gentle looking face, she didn't panic. He bowed slightly from the waist as he entered the room, and without saying a word he picked up a brush or pencil and stepped behind a large canvas.

After sitting patiently for several minutes, she wanted to speak to him, but for the first time in years she did not know what to say.

Finally, what came out of her mouth was "Hello. What am I doing here?"

The little artist smiled broadly and responded in Spanish, and although she spoke no language other than English, she recognized it the way any Floridian would have. At least that culture hadn't embraced stoning since the inquisition, so that concern was addressed.[*]

"I didn't know you could speak English my madonna," he said from behind the large canvas. "You are here because I am paying you."

Crystal quickly dismissed the fear that she might be considered a prostitute in favor of the

---

[*] She was actually in Paris, which she would have learned if she had made it to the street.

obvious, that she was posing for a fee. Sensing his model's agitation, the little artist put his brush down and went into the other room. He returned with a glass of red wine, which she accepted from his hand although the exchange took a bit too long. He then reached as if to reposition her by moving her shoulder slightly, but his hand dropped slowly and intentionally across her breast.

    Well I could have told him what a bad idea that was, having seen Crystal administer justice to uninvited fondlers more than once, but this guy wasn't accustomed to refusals, so he was unprepared for her reflexive violence. As he lay writhing on the ground, she roughly unbuttoned his shirt, jerked it from his shoulders and threw it across her body as she stormed through the house looking for something else to wear. During this short search, she swatted paintings from walls and launched pottery out of windows, so the neighbors soon became aware of the disturbance and began to assemble outside. That would signal the end of Crystal's sojourn into the world of fine art.

    I was still pressing Nachron about the blurry transparency that had replaced my friend when her vague image began to reappear. We heard coughing and retching before the corporeal Crystal had fully materialized, but the first appendages to come into sharp focus were her forearms and hands, which seemed to be closing ominously on the silverware. Several of the patrons and two of the waiters had now begun to stare at the confusion at our table, which until that moment, had escaped notice. Crystal, now fully reassembled, burst onto the scene alternately spewing and snarling, so I grabbed Nachron and lifted him out of his chair to protect him from the potentially dangerous and repulsive vision unfolding before us. As the waiters scowled contemptuously in our direction, Crystal rose from the soiled table like dark vengeance. She growled at us with her hair laying in wet clumps across her face as she waved a serrated knife in our direction.

"If you two ever put me through anything like that again, I will carve one of my initials in each of your chests."

Nachron stared at me helplessly, but I knew what to do from here: a towel and a taxi for Crystal after some soothing words, apologies to the other patrons, who weren't sure of what they'd seen, and big tips for the waiters who had to cope with the clutter of our spoiled evening. During the drive back to his apartment, Nachron was subdued. He was mumbling to himself, questioning his own judgment regarding Crystal's experience and vowing not to repeat his mistake.

I couldn't get much more out of him until we got home, where we attempted to relive the evening from Crystal's perspective.

"I blame myself," he began "for the failure to anticipate Señor Picasso's concupiscence as well as the vigor of her response. Her destruction of so many works of art gives the notion of unintended consequences painful clarity, does it not?"

"Do you mean," I indignantly blurted, "that the lecherous little troll tried to mount her?"

He frowned, but patiently continued. "The entire sequence of occurrences explains something that has puzzled me for some time. At some stage in his career, after depicting countless subjects in his work realistically or nearly so, Picasso embraced the angular surrealism that was to become his trademark. Crystal, with her volatile nature, might have been the catalyst in that creative transformation. She was, I now believe, the inspiration for his first spasm of geometric anger at the human form."

All I could think to say was: "Are you telling me that the little satyr tried to climb aboard my friend?"

"Your peculiar form of protectiveness," he said, "is unnecessary. She is obviously quite capable of defending herself, so there is no need to sulk. There is one noteworthy item I will share with you, however. Crystal's portrait will one day hang in the Museum of Modern Art in New York, where it will be recognized as the earliest and most visceral of its genre. For now, the painting is in the collection of a reclusive admirer of Cubism."

I had a pretty good idea who that collector might be, but I didn't intend to give Nachron the opportunity to gloat, so I went to bed.

Mike Corbett

TWELVE

Having recently made the upward transition to a Las Olas penthouse, I was beginning to become more aware of my surroundings. For instance, I noticed that when Albert Nachron paced silently for more than a few seconds, it would mean I was to be offered another exceptional opportunity. He even troubled himself to bring a glass of iced tea from the kitchen and ask me if I had slept well, so I knew there would soon be a full canteen and a bon voyage in my future.

"Since your trip to Panama, I sense a growing enthusiasm for Spanish language and culture. Is this so?"

I knew what Mr. Nachron's words were intended to accomplish. He assumed that since I had sat around long enough without risking my health or sanity, I might be ripe for another one of his imaginative proposals. Since I didn't respond quickly enough, nor did I have time to adjust the vacant look on my face, he was encouraged to continue.

"If I could once again suggest that you would not have to concern yourself with threats of physical violence, I wonder if you could be persuaded to do another small favor for me."

"What does my enthusiasm for Spanish have to do with it; am I to learn how to dance the Flamenco?" I had answered his question with one of my own, but he continued undeterred.

"As you are by now aware, once I become curious about some relatively esoteric item, I do not rest comfortably until I know its nature. There is no chance that the object I seek will be what its possessor claims, but the circumstances are such, as I hope you will soon perceive, to warrant an investigation."

We walked out on the large balcony, which had a great view of the city with Port Everglades and the sea in the background. Once comfortably seated, he talked for two hours about the fifteenth century exploits of Christopher Columbus with the sovereign support of Ferdinand and Isabella.*

After the first twenty minutes, I had the suspicion that I might be going on a transatlantic cruise, and if you put any faith in historical records, there was misery enough for every man jack during that expedition. Nachron eventually got around to describing my expected role in his latest production,

---

* Although Ferdinand and Isabella are best remembered for their sponsorship of Columbus, they should also be held at least partially responsible for the cruelty of the Inquisition, which could not have happened without their approval.

and it seemed that Columbus was intended to sail without me. His expectation would limit my service to the mainland. I was destined for the Iberian Peninsula, where I was to use my ingenuity in procuring a small vial full of an unknown substance. He recommended that I begin my search in Seville and travel from there as circumstances might dictate, and he quickly agreed to my request for a bag of gold coins to facilitate the project. My first serious misgiving arose when he presented me the next day with the costume I was expected to wear in order to fit in.

I should have known when I saw the plain coarse robe that there was a cloud on my horizon, but I just wasn't clever enough to identify it. If I had been familiar enough with fifteenth century Spanish history, I might have connected the simple robe I was to wear with the Dominican Order and thus the notorious Inquisition. You may have assumed that as a member of a religious order, I would have enjoyed relative immunity from some of the injustices visited on Muslims and Jews by the true believers. In fact, I was to learn that along with the resentment the specific community subjected to torture may have for its oppressors, there was a conspiracy of whispers even among presumably innocent Christians that was turning them against one another.

Nachron once again gave me his promise that no harm would befall me, so I went into my bedroom and tried on the robe. I must admit that before I went to sleep that night, I posed in front of the mirror with what I thought was the appropriate demeanor for an archbishop. I stood staring admiringly with waist cord tied and untied, sometimes with a benedictory hand raised to bless my invisible flock. This exercise of self-appreciation was sufficiently soporific to guarantee that I remained unconscious for my trip to Spain.

"Every saint has a past and every sinner has a future"
Oscar Wilde

THIRTEEN

Spain

I wasn't exactly an archbishop. My quarters were dark and smaller than a prison cell without decent ventilation or a recognizable toilet, so I was compelled to exit the premises to relieve myself. I was obviously not even a full-blown monk, since my duties seemed to alternate between washing the feet of the holier folks and emptying their slop jars. I was just a trainee, and if that weren't humiliating enough, some of the brothers kept pulling at my robe so they could hear my confession in their cubicles. I was once told by a female acquaintance that she could read the sins of my past in my eyes, so maybe that was happening here. In any event, I wasn't going to be tempted into candle lit privacy so a holy man could hear my sins or practice his on me. It was not yet perfectly clear to me that there might be significant benefits to absolute anonymity, so my behavior during the first few days, while not yet damnable, had begun to attract the notice of a few of the suspicious elders.

Admittedly, my liturgical Latin was a bit weak and my Calle Ocho Spanish was confusing to the ears of some of the doddering old Castilian clerics, but I still trusted my ability to fly below the radar. I patiently awaited my opportunity to slip into the rooms of the head of the tribunal that directed my life and return with a small vial full of the mysterious powder Nachron had described.

In the meantime, the principal authority of that tribunal, The Grand Inquisitor Tomás de Torquemada, was traveling in and out of Seville listening to rumors and setting people on fire in the name of God. Since my duties as a foot scrubber rarely brought me out into the civilian population, I never had the privilege of witnessing any of the more than two thousand executions Torquemada choreographed, but I did secretly eavesdrop on some of the interrogations. They were solemn affairs, held in almost total darkness so that the accused couldn't look directly into the faces of the pious hypocrites who might condemn him.

It's possible that some of these unfortunate wretches were guilty of something, but in general, the only crime the Muslims and Jews who were victimized by this farce were guilty of was to behave like Christians so unconvincingly that Tomás and his buddies felt obliged to discipline them. The punishments were quite severe. If you could not convince the questioner that you had totally abandoned the religion of your fathers in favor of Christianity, you might be sent to burn at the stake.* If enough people whispered about you, the rumors might also be enough to inculpate, but Master Torquemada directly or indirectly authorized all of the butchery.

He never traveled without guards, and he became increasingly paranoid as the number of his enemies multiplied, so he was going to be very difficult to sneak up on. The item I required, according to Nachron, was always beside his bed as he slept. The rest of the time he kept it in a secret pocket in his undergarment so he could feel its reassuring pressure against his skin. I knew the guards would become suspicious if I started groping around in Torquemada's underwear in the daytime, so I elected to make a nocturnal assault.

Getting into his room was easier than I thought thanks to the purse full of gold coins I had distributed. It turns out that men of the cloth are just as easy to bribe as politicians, but I was cautious not to assume that once bribed, they would give fair value. I quietly darted down the darkly lit hallway that led to the Grand Inquisitor's chamber and tested the door. It was no surprise to find it unlocked, since he probably felt safe in the bosom of the brotherhood, but the room seemed to have no occupant so I let my guard down to study its contents. On a small table next to the bed was what I hoped was the little container I was sent for, but as I walked around the unnecessarily large

---

* There were a surprising number of ways to burn someone at the stake. The most merciful, a reward for recanting, was to kill the accused before the fire was lit. The cruelest was to use green slow burning wood which would prolong the event.

bed where he slept, an alarming doubt occurred to me. If the vial he always kept by his side was here, where was Torquemada? As I snatched the object from the table, I felt the tip of something very sharp being held somewhat unsteadily to my neck.

"Good evening brother," he whispered. "God has answered my prayers. When I saw you stealing the antidote, I knew you were sent to save my immortal soul."

He removed the knife from my neck and walked slowly around to face me, turning the little blade around and offering it to me with the handle extended. When he turned his back to me and dropped his robe to expose his bare skin, I saw that he intended for me to break a commandment. I later learned that Torquemada had not been sleeping for some time due to the many visions of suffering that intruded on his thoughts. This should not have been surprising since he had not only authorized the executions of entire innocent families, he even had to endure the inconvenience of witnessing a few personally.

Since he was intent on saving his own soul, and in view of the fact that suicide was believed to be a one-way ticket to hell, he had been praying that his life would end sometime between his evening confession and the horrors of the following morning. The little vial that I still clasped in the other hand was purported to contain a quantity of the only known antidote to all of the world's poisons. He had made a habit of sniffing a tiny bit of this grainy substance, which was supposed to be the powdered horn of a unicorn, every day to counteract the effects of some toxin that might be introduced into his food, but his steadily increasing feelings of guilt had only recently caused him to give up that habit.

He stood before me with his pale flabby back heaving as he sobbed what he thought would be his expiration prayer while I considered my own moral dilemma. If I threw the knife down and escaped into the street, I could probably count on Nachron to snatch me back without my having to take the life of a fellow human being. If on the other hand, I skewered the trembling beast before me in the middle of his mea culpas, I might save countless lives that would be in danger if he survived the moment. Luckily, before I had time to weigh the merits of justifiable homicide, Nachron spirited me away with the unicorn dust still in my hand. The last words I spoke in Spain were "ad inferno tecum", but they gave no hint of my intentions.

I ignored Nachron's welcoming speech as I swerved by him to get into the shower. There's something about the combination of torture, religion, and the contemplation of homicide that made me feel dirty, and if that weren't enough to justify some abrasive cleaning, I couldn't get the smell of monk's foot off my hands for days. I tossed him the little vial as I sped by him, and he rushed off somewhere to give it a proper testing. We met in the living room some time later after I had time to put the robe into a garbage bag and scrub my flesh pink. He seemed satisfied with himself for solving the unicorn mystery, but I couldn't resist his need to unravel the entire story for me, so I settled myself on the couch and prepared for the inevitable monologue.

"I assumed at first that the vial contained the powdered horn of a rhinoceros, which is not actually horn but hair as I'm sure you know, but there was far too much calcium in the substance to be bristles or hair. The rhinoceros was unfamiliar to most Europeans at that time, but it was close enough to some primitive conceptions of a unicorn as to prompt unscrupulous merchants to offer it as a panacea. After pondering the issue for a bit, I concluded that the material within that vial was a finely ground human coccyx, somehow extracted from the embers of one of the executions. Furthermore, the unwilling donor of that substance was the uncle of the Jewish merchant who successfully misrepresented it. Would you call that irony?"

I called it sickening. Torquemada was tricked into snorting the butt bone of a supposedly heretical Jew. Even the historians, if they knew the truth, would be challenged to treat that subject with delicacy.

The next morning, while I remained in an exhausted sleep, Mr. Nachron went to a local synagogue and gave the vial to a rabbi, with the information he would need to act according to tradition.

FOURTEEN

I had so many tantalizing questions about the new direction of my life that they were starting to outnumber my doubts. Anxiety was being displaced by a sense of wonder. Plausible fear was losing ground to mere hesitation. In short, it seemed more and more likely that Nachron's choice of errand boys was reasonable. I was selected, he said, because my behavior around strangers, friendly and otherwise, was sufficiently natural as not to arouse undue curiosity or suspicion. I could be clever without seeming superior, physically capable without being intimidating, resourceful without appearing sneaky, and as Nachron tactlessly put it, I was neither handsome nor hideous but occupied some inconspicuous middle ground. Most importantly, he continued, I had an appetite for life and its many challenges and rewards.

I would never have described myself as a thrill seeker since I am more than a little frightened by excessive speed or heights. For example, I would not even board one of those rickety propeller-driven planes that take sky divers up for a hundred bucks, much less jump out the door at however many thousands of feet. There are only two possible consequences of such an act. Gravity either sucks you back to earth fast enough to pulverize all of your body parts, or your descent is slowed sufficiently to limit your injuries to an occasional sprain or concussion. If there were just a few more options that weren't life-threatening I might reconsider, but compared to spelunking around in Mr. Nachron's temporal maze, bungee cords and mountain climbing were comparatively unattractive.

On the question of how I might prepare myself for the potential hazards of my assignments, Nachron said I could bring almost anything I chose, as long as it wasn't too large. When I asked him about a hand gun or a taser, he inquired about my level of experience with same, and I had to confess I had little.

"It seems that the person most likely to come to harm if I indulge this impulse of yours, is yourself" he volunteered. "Perhaps you should reconsider."

He proposed the obvious utility of bringing a few small denomination gold coins and a phrase book to help me spend them sensibly. After dismissing many of my suggestions such as a thermal-imaging sniper rifle and a gob of plastique explosive, he agreed to allow me to bring a bar of soap and a small quantity of a powerful antibiotic.

This might simultaneously enable me to cure myself and to potentially seem like a great healer to someone in need of relief from a simple infection.

As for my choice of attire, the emphasis would be on cotton and leather, avoiding bright colors and combinations thereof. There is a long history of cultural sensitivity to certain color schemes among families, tribes, clans, and other groups of primates, and I did not wish to be unintentionally offensive. Simplicity in muted or faded tones wouldn't necessarily guarantee anonymity, but except for my height (6'2"), I could blend into a crowd if I avoided tassels and other such appurtenances. Thus, with certain necessary adaptations, such as appropriately-dated currency, I felt I could go almost anywhere.

My most valuable asset, according to my elfin travel agent, was a superbly honed sense of self-preservation. The sound of a hammer on a pistol of any vintage clicking back would put me to flight precious moments before the actual sound of a weapon being fired. I could also sense anger in its nascent state, and when I anticipated its direction and magnitude, I instinctively knew how to avoid it, with one exception. Apparently, I can look into a woman's eyes without being able to differentiate between simple boredom and revulsion. I bear several psychological scars as testimony to that weakness, but I guess I'll always be an optimist.

Thanks to Albert Nachron, I had also gained a number of new and useful perspectives. Along with the obvious benefits that accrue as a consequence of experience and maturity, I was treated to the tactical insights of a truly remarkable mind. In the evenings that I spent in his company, we played chess and backgammon, seldom without Mozart or Gershwin's music in the background. In fact, there was a Gershwin-like composition that I did not recognize, so I asked about its source. He chuckled knowingly and said that it did not live up to both brothers' high standards, so Ira threw it away. I was learning by that time to suppress my curiosity about his possessions, so reluctantly, I let it drop.

His tactical insights over a game board were so useful that they could eventually help me learn how to deal with many of life's obstacles. Very generally, he instructed me to weigh carefully the benefits of the reward that would justify even moderate risk, and then act accordingly. He made me aware of the line of least resistance and the justifications for ignoring it. He explained this counterintuitive idea by assuring me that the most brilliant chess players would never have learned the game if they weren't capable of occasionally avoiding a conservative strategy in favor of a daring and imaginative one.

As he put it; "If you cannot anticipate the shortcomings of an unfamiliar idea, the failure of similar notions will multiply somewhere else to thwart you."

He was making a case, to paraphrase, for going outside of your comfort zone if the result of doing so included exposure to otherwise inaccessible information.

FIFTEEN

I don't know if he watched me as I slept, but he always seem to know when I woke up.

"Good morning my friend. You look remarkably fit this morning. I trust you slept well, and if you have an appetite, I have taken the liberty of ordering a grand breakfast from my favorite restaurant with seasonal fruits and other delicacies to tempt the palate."

By then, I was awake enough to sense that I was being buttered up for another caper, but I was slowly losing my reluctance to do Nachron's bidding, so he needn't have wasted his persuasive abilities. To be perfectly honest, the lazy pace of a few days lolling around Chez Nachron, followed by wild dashes through time, was producing an addictive rhythm to which I was yielding.

Having honored his various requests, I had looked forward to the promised rewards, but I was not prepared for his next suggestion.

"Ronny," he began, "I wondered if you might be receptive to a bit of deviation from your former efforts. I hoped you might enjoy a little vacation without the burden of having to seek out and bring back some little trinket. It might add a new dimension to our mutual experiences."

I should have been paying closer attention to his choice of words, since he so rarely wasted one, but I might have had one too many glasses of champagne with the kiwi mousse so I missed the obvious hint he offered. He also mentioned something about the relative unimportance of pie, with which I heartily agreed, since it would have clashed with the excellent mousse.

The long and entertaining conversation continued into the evening, and Nachron with another of his surprises, turned up with a pan of fresh wahoo steaks topped by a mango sauce. This, along with a dazzling Meursault, was all the prompting I would need to agree to anything he wished, so I don't have to explain in detail what happened after I got drowsy.

"Two roads diverged in a wood and I - I took the one less traveled by."   Robert Frost

SIXTEEN

The Matrix

    I couldn't really say when or even if I had regained consciousness, but it wasn't Kansas anymore. I tried to inventory my senses one by one to establish a frame of reference, but aside from a vague feeling of well-being, I had no recognizable context to focus on. What kind of stimuli could Nachron have planned for me in what seemed like a state of suspended animation?

    In the ordinary world that I had left, I had always felt somewhat disconnected. Wherever I now existed, I enjoyed a strange feeling of comfort at the orderly, systematic impulses that were growing within me as time passed. I even had what seemed like a visual hallucination, the entirety of which was a matrix of regressive geometric structures, somehow pleasingly parallel. What the hell was I thinking about? I'm not even sure what I was doing was thinking since my feet and arms were nowhere to be found, and the thing I had apparently become was not even vaguely human. It would have been frightening if I did not have full confidence in Nachron's ability to rescue me from this geometry lesson that was supposed to be a relief from my humdrum duties.

Once I realized that there was no immediate threat to my health or comfort, I started thinking about how to interact in this challenging new setting. At first, I projected simple ideas like "hallooo" and "friend", which seemed to reverberate away and then back through me. On the return trip, the echoes of my own thoughts were accompanied by question marks or their sensory equivalent. What did that mean? This tepid response emboldened me to experiment further. I started mentally screaming phrases like "ecce homo" and "cogito ergo sum" because I was losing patience with the futility of my efforts.

The only idea which got a different reaction was a clue that I now realized Nachron had given me. I clenched my nonexistent teeth and concentrated on 3.14, which I mentally repeated a number of times. The response to that was a small but detectable tremor that seemed to affect all of my neighbors as it did me. I felt like "the ugly American" whose voice had suddenly become too loud as the other diners looked disapprovingly in my direction. Maybe I would postpone my idea of emitting sequences of prime numbers until I was sure I wasn't the guest who had overstayed his welcome.

After an indeterminate period, I found myself becoming slowly acclimated to these strange new surroundings. The absolute uniformity of my environment was less tedious then you might assume, as there was also no threat of hostility or discomfort, and the whole community, if that's what it could be called, was in obvious harmony. Occasionally, a pleasing chill would pass through my structure, enhancing my sense of satisfying communion with my fellows on either side and above and below me.

Just as I was comfortably settling into a total absence of autonomy, something happened that would have floored me if I were still a biped. Through the colorless matrix that extended in every direction, I became aware of a two dimensional little pink triangle zigzagging erratically toward me. To witness the intrusion of color and movement so suddenly and unexpectedly was disconcerting to say the least, but what happened next filled me with pleasure.

Have you ever walked through a park with a friend and had a butterfly land on you momentarily, slowly beating its wings in the sunlight, living its short life unaware of the nature of the surface upon which it rests? If you remain still enough so as not to frighten it, then you can't help but feel a sense of happiness that you have been given the privilege of offering hospitality to this creature, and that was the sensation I experienced here. In what felt like moments, that lovely pink thing was joined by others with various angular configurations that seemed to arrive from every direction. It was like standing in St. Mark's Square among a crowd of tourists and having a mob of brightly colored creatures single you out to honor, except in Venice it would be the unpleasant attention of pigeons. You will no doubt recoil at my apparent vanity, but I felt I was as never before the object of veneration.

While this was all happening, I failed to notice that some of my fellow polygons seemed to be slowly retreating. The blissful unitary sensation that I had previously noted was receding as well, and I wondered what the consequences of such a phenomenon would be. Had I unwittingly traded order and satisfaction for the momentary pleasures of a butterfly? Well, I've done things like that before, and I'm sure I'm not alone. As long as these playful pink things surrounded me though, I was prepared to bask in their attention just like any common hedonist.

This was seeming more and more like a real vacation. My new existence was happily free of automated marketing solicitations and drive-by shootings, allowing me the leisure to fully appreciate bliss; or so I thought. The tantalizing pink delights couldn't completely remove the intensifying sensation of isolation as the empty space around me continued to grow. I didn't have the luxury of too much reflection, because I could feel the now familiar pull of Nachron's will, drawing me back to Fort Lauderdale.

SEVENTEEN

Nachron's curious expression was the first thing to come into focus as my confusion gradually subsided. He seemed only moderately concerned as he observed the return of my faculties, but I woozily anticipated his compulsion to enlighten me. Since we were still sitting on his couch in the living room, I asked him how long I'd been absent or unconscious, or whatever. His response would have surprised most people, but I was unfazed.

"Although I didn't measure it exactly, I estimate the length of your stay to have been something less than a fifth of a second. Did it seem a bit too long?"

I was still uncertain of what had happened during my so-called vacation, so I inquired about the nature of that strange environment and its occupants, knowing that my credibility anywhere but in this room would likely be challenged.

"Ronny," he began, "you are the first of your kind to realize man's dream of visiting another dimension. Did you appreciate the irrelevance of time and space? Were you surprised by the ease with which you shed the confinements of your species? If it weren't for the unanticipated fluctuation in your temperature, I may have permitted you to extend your stay a bit, but consistent with your nature, you tend to cause a tumult wherever you go. I understand that it was through no fault of your own, but you were creating discomfort among a great many of the hmm.... let's call them residents."

Since I thought I had behaved like a model citizen in that unfamiliar environment, I implored him to elaborate further.

"My boy," he continued, "Did you notice the absolute stereotypy of your surroundings? In order to precisely insert you into that dimension, it was necessary for you to assume the appropriate form to mix with the indigenous population. Your temperature was lowered to absolute zero, and for the first time in your life you were superconductive, which means electromagnetic impulses could pass through you at close to the speed of light. Was that not a thrill? The cause of the disturbance was your thermal reaction to the arrival of those autonomous impulses that may have seemed pink to you. You reacted so pleasurably to their fondling that your temperature rose by almost a billionth of a degree, which produced a sequence of events that you must have noticed among your immediate neighbors.

"Since you were so clearly different, and thus a possible threat to the fabric of their existence, those nearest you collectively began to shrink away. Unfortunately, this movement involved such structural deformation in order to create room around you that a nearly round space was created as a buffer, and this could not be tolerated. Do you remember me informing you about the irrelevance of pi? With the sudden appearance of spatial curvature, previously unknown in that dimension, it was necessary to extract you. There is no telling what sort of chaos I would have been responsible for if I had permitted that chain reaction to persist."

"So Mr. Nachron," I asked, "Other than a fraction of a degree of heat, what impressions did I leave in that place?"

"In order to produce a plausible comparison for you, I will rely on your ability to conceptualize. To the geometric uniformity that you warmly adopted as your new family, you were an incomprehensible horror, unfamiliar and unbearably hot."

"What about those pink things?" I asked. "They seemed to like me."

"Well Ronny," he responded. "I thought you knew. To them you were God."

After sharing that surprising insight with me, he told me he had something further to show me and went to the bedroom to find it. He spent five minutes shuffling around through one of his oversized cabinets before returning with what appeared to be some kind of bronze plaque, partially oxidized by exposure to the elements. He held it before him so I could read the inscribed words: "If there is no hell, many of your neighbors in heaven will be unendurable." For all I knew, this wisdom could have been torn from the gravestone of

Oscar Wilde or a memorial to Mark Twain, but I really had no reason to know how he happened to come by his prize, so I remained silent. "I just thought that this memento was relevant to our conversation," he said, "and as to the origin of the words upon it, I believe they can be traced to a work called *Laughter of the Damned* by a relatively unknown author. The most tempting challenges to a fertile imagination revolve around what we call the supernatural, do they not?"

I spent the rest of that day and a good part of the next thinking about heaven, hell, and Nachron. If this guy enjoyed the universal access he seemed to possess, he might have insights that would tantalize popes and imams. Late that afternoon, Nachron popped his head into my room and asked if I might enjoy a little stroll, and a walk on Las Olas toward the beach around sunset was hard to resist. I broached the subject nonchalantly as we walked.

"Albert, the other day we were talking about the supernatural and I was wondering, among other things, if there's a hell."

We walked thirty paces in silence before he looked at me with a peculiar expression.

"You may have underestimated my limitations," he said. "It may seem to you that life and death, heaven and hell, and concepts like an immortal soul are separate issues. I would not knowingly discourage you from that belief, but has it occurred to you that suffering similar to that which may be found in hell and innocence that must exist in heaven can be simultaneously found in the eyes of a starving child?"

"Hell is a more graphic and threatening concept, so it gets most of the interesting publicity, but heaven is wonderfully vague and may be beyond the reach of even the aspirations of the pious. It is not my intention to confuse you, but if your experiences with me have been of any value, you must know that not only are all such ideas many things to many people. They are many things to every person, with eternity having no more or less value than a nanosecond. If you live your life as if the devil were a poisonous beast behind you and heaven stood with open gates in front of you, you won't go too far wrong. The removal of the traditional barrier of time has permitted me insights few creatures have, but for every certainty regarding my particular existence, there are scores of unanswered questions. To your eyes, I suspect I seem evolved. To others, I am as primitive as a mollusk."

Mike Corbett

EIGHTEEN

The Party

It is pleasant to put the sun at your back as you walk to the beach in the late afternoon, and then arrange your return to coincide with its setting. If I timed it perfectly, I might even catch Crystal arriving at the beginning of her shift and spend an hour with her before dinner. When I left the apartment, Nachron was nowhere to be seen, so I was surprised when he stuck his head in the door only moments after I had entered Murray's and waved a greeting to Crystal and me.

"Ah, my dear friends, I'm glad I caught you. I was wondering if you and Crystal would help me arrange a small party. It would be nice if we could have a variety of special wines, and I believe the two of you are capable of finding a few selections that would impress the guests. Are you interested?"

I looked at Crystal, who nodded her consent since we both knew from experience that Nachron would be a charming and generous host. Also, it would be fun going around to the liquor stores and dickering with the managers to reduce the prices on some of their fancier vintages. Nachron beamed when we agreed to help him, and then he excused himself saying he had arrangements to make, and presumably returned to his apartment.

Crystal was already on the phone getting someone to cover her shift on the night of the party, and I was making a mental itinerary of liquor stores we would visit in order to fill A.N.'s order. We were told that the event was to be in two days, so we decided to start our hunt the next morning, without stopping until we had chosen enough wine to entertain thirteen discerning palates. I also spent some time wondering what the other guests would be like, since I had mistakenly assumed that we were Albert's only friends.

By nine o'clock the next evening, we had purchased almost six thousand dollars worth of exceptional wines. Many were California reds since that's what we knew best, but we included a mixture of French reds and whites as well as a couple of surprises from Chile and Australia. Twenty-seven bottles of wine for thirteen people in one evening seemed like overkill, but Nachron had told us to spare no expense, and if a bottle or two weren't opened, we could find some use for it in the future.

In any event, Nachron didn't even blink when he saw what we had spent. His only reaction was to thank us and tell us to prepare for an evening of games and music, and that he would provide a few snacks.

I spent the night before Nachron's grand affair at Murray's Pub discussing the possibilities with Crystal. Would everybody look like the host? Maybe even the women would be pale and peculiar, but there was one certainty. If they were his friends, it would be a fascinating group. I agreed to pick her up the next evening after I helped Nachron prepare the apartment for guests, and one beer later I took the short walk back up Las Olas to my temporary home.

When the night of the party arrived, I drove to Crystal's apartment building to find her waiting near the entrance. She hopped into the car before I could open the door for her, giving my arm a friendly squeeze as she put on her seat belt. She looked great, she smelled great, and when the valet opened the car door at Chez Nachron, his eyes never left her until we reached the elevator. The only problem with having a friend that pretty was that other girls would assume you were unavailable, and because of my obsession with Lynn, maybe that was just as well.

I was surprised when we entered Nachron's apartment that all the other guests were already there. I couldn't have been away for more than twenty minutes, so these folks must have arrived very shortly after my departure. Stranger still, not one of them looked anything like Nachron. The room was alive with the laughter and conversation of youngish attractive people who graciously smiled a welcome as Crystal preceded me into their midst.

We each received a glass of wine and introductions to the other guests before separating over the hors d'oeuvres table. Albert, true to his promise, had concocted an elaborate array of tempting offerings. The only thing on my plate I could confidently identify was a mushroom. Everything else was colorfully mysterious, hinting vaguely of lime or raspberry with a smear of glaze over something on a cracker. There was one sautéed fish filet that produced the familiar memory of a conversation we had with Nachron about chicken. While I was contemplating this, an attractive guy that had been staring at Crystal since we walked in was sharing his opinions about wine with her, so I decided to do a little mingling.

    I moved to the center of the room, where a man and a woman were sitting down at a large chess board and beginning to set up the pieces. I did not at first notice the electronic-looking panel it was mounted on, but there are sophisticated programs that can be adapted to track play, so I assumed that was the case here. But it was way more than that. When a white pawn was touched, tall Gothic projections of each of the pieces appeared as holograms over the board. As the pawn was moved it became animated, making me think I had underestimated the advances that 21st century program designers were capable of. I was even more amazed when a knight, made lifelike with its first touch, captured a pawn. It did so by pushing a sword through the middle of its victim, spinning it on the blade twice and flipping it end-over-end to the side of the board. Equally surprising to me was the grisly sound that the pawn made as it was impaled, like an overripe tomato being thrown against a wall. I could've drunk great wine and watched chess like this for hours, but I wanted to make sure Crystal wasn't trapped in some boring conversation, so I unsuccessfully surveyed the room looking for her.

    I eventually located her on the balcony, obviously enjoying the company of a beautiful girl who might have been the youngest guest. The single distraction from her striking appearance was a pair of glasses with very thick lenses that suggested a severe vision handicap. I had never seen Crystal so comfortable with a new acquaintance, but the Château Margaux she was drinking probably contributed to her merry disposition, so I went back inside to enjoy the party. The other guests were so excited about the array of libations that they heaped praise on their host, and by extension on me. I thought they might be overdoing it a little, but too much politeness is a forgivable excess, so I poured another glass.

The next time I looked at the holographic images over the chess board, the black king was falling on his own sword, terminating the visual display. Nachron allowed the light applause to subside before he went to the balcony to escort the nearly blind girl back into the room.

"Jennifer," he announced as he returned, "has graciously agreed to share her remarkable gift with us this evening. If you would fill your glasses and find a comfortable seat, I will promise you something memorable."

Nachron went into another room and brought back what appeared to be a very fine old violin case which he opened, carefully passing the instrument into Jennifer's waiting hands. She nimbly and quickly tuned it as the room became silent with expectation, but when she drew the bow across the strings producing the first tone, there was enchantment.

I don't know enough about classical music to identify all the notable composers and their work, but it didn't matter at all after about ten seconds, to me or anyone else in the room. Jennifer wasn't just holding a violin in her arms. She had gathered all twelve of us into her embrace and carried us with her into her pain, her passion, and ultimately her joy. No one cared how much time had passed, but if the minutes could be measured by the intervals between the flow and the drying of tears before eyes became moist again, it was quite a while.

You would think a performance like that would earn a lot of applause, but it didn't happen that night. Each guest went silently up to the beautiful musician to hug her and make a personal expression of gratitude in private, so Crystal and I did the same. Maybe this was the way they did it in Europe. In any event, no party could have survived the terrible void that followed Jennifer's artistry, so people began to hug each other, thank the host and move toward the door. Nachron proposed that I take Crystal home and he would see the guest of honor out after thanking her again, but Crystal and Jennifer weren't easy to separate. As Nachron and I stood back to permit their final embrace, they held hands so tightly that their fingertips whitened. It was touching, but a little odd that they would have bonded so quickly.

I put my arm around Crystal in the elevator but she didn't even notice it.

"I hope," she said, "I will be able to hear her play again some day."

With Nachron, I never knew what was possible, so I didn't promise her that there would be an encore. I just squeezed her shoulder and patted her arm until the valet brought my car.

Since she was so quiet on the way to her apartment, I decided to give her the benefit of my sophisticated masculine perspective. I told her how every average guy dreams about a beautiful talented blind girl, since she can't tell how plain he is unless he has warts or smells bad. Ugly is hard to feel with your fingertips, so everybody has a shot. Also, it is unlikely she would run away with the pool boy because of his abs or tan. Crystal emitted an eloquent sigh of disgust and let her head flop backwards against the car seat. I knew she wasn't thinking how clever and sensitive I was, so I shared no more of my wisdom with her.

  I was anxious to return to Nachron's place quickly because I didn't want to forget any of the questions that were nagging at me. I was hoping Crystal didn't notice my impatience as I walked her to her door and jumped back in my car for the return trip.

  When I got back, Nachron was alone admiring the color of a wine that I hadn't sampled, so he invited me to join him. Before I could start badgering him, he waved me into a chair and began speaking.

  "Our guests were almost as thrilled with your wine choices as they were with the music. It was a great success. If you were thinking about their strange arrivals and departures, let's just say they didn't use the elevator, and as you have probably already guessed (I hadn't), they are more a part of the next few decades than they are of this one. Like you, they are curious enough to test their temporal versatility. Did you notice them raving about the vintages? (I had). As the climate of the entire planet changes, there will be a price to pay and I'm afraid that part of the bill will fall to the world's wine producers. Varietal grapes will become impossible to cultivate very soon, and I'm sorry to tell you that only the wealthiest Chinese oligarchs will have had the foresight to stockpile fine wine. The prices will be well above what you have spent on tonight's festivities, and accessibility, even to the most dreadful vintages, will be extremely limited."

"So, do you mean," I asked "that I won't even be able to get a jug of dumpster wine in a few years?"

"Dumpster wine," he remarked, "is not familiar to me. Is it admirable?"

I described in some detail the variables that dictated the necessity for drinking dumpster wine. First: it cannot be consumed by anyone who is not desperate. Second: it cannot be enjoyed unless it is preceded by a sufficient amount of another intoxicant to render the consumer nearly insensate. Third: it is best enjoyed with an equally unfortunate friend who might not notice he is leaning beside you against a receptacle full of smelly garbage.

Nachron's response was a shudder and a grimace, after which he left the room.

I said to his retreating form: "What about that violin? Was it a Strad?"

He neither answered nor did he return. The thought of dumpster wine must have been too much for him, so I'll probably never get the story of that chess board either.

NINETEEN

A History Lesson

After a restless night's sleep and a hot breakfast provided by my grateful host, I was treated to a preview of what would possibly be my next trip.

"If you are not already excited by this chapter in your nation's history, your next sojourn should be delightfully informative."

Nachron was referring to the Civil War, and nothing I remember from my history classes implied anything delightful, but my silence encouraged him to continue.

"Have you not envied the seafaring man with sharp eyes trained on an unknown horizon, reveling in the bosom of fellowship with like minded heroic sorts?"

If I needed to expel the contents of my stomach, I might have endured this presentation, but I had to remind him of scurvy, mutiny, and other dangers too numerous to mention, not the least of which was drowning. He applauded my sensible reluctance, but then asked the following question.

"If you had to take some small part in the War Between the States, would you prefer to serve in the infantry or navy?"

Well if you put it that way, I assumed that the casualty rate for sailors from either side was relatively small, so I conceded the point.

"Perhaps," he said, "this missive will help you to familiarize yourself with one of the principal characters in the next adventure in which you will be lucky enough to participate."

He had in his hand an old looking envelope with a postmark and stamp consistent with the war years and "U.S. Ship" stamped diagonally across the cancellation. Inside it was what looked like an age-yellowed piece of personal correspondence, which he asked me to read and reread for my edification. The following is an abbreviated version of that letter, and although I have changed some of the names of those involved for privacy's sake, I trust I have faithfully retained the information therein. I had a bit of difficulty with the handwriting and usage, but you may be the judge of the document's believability. Why Nachron thought this letter would induce me to sign on for his project I couldn't guess, but perhaps he knew me better than I knew myself, since once more against my better judgment, I was being drawn into his plans.

Off Charleston S.C.
Sept. 4, 1864
Iron Clad Sangamon

Capt. L. P. Johnson
c/o Peter W. Neefos Esq.
231 W. Street
Newark, N. J.

Dear Johnson,

Yours at the 23rd of August reached me a few days ago and it did me good to hear from you. I am glad to hear our signal arrangements are doing so well and hope soon to hear of a favorable report. I am confident that it will be received with favor in merchant service and agree with you that under the circumstances it will be better to not be in a hurry.......... The great difficulty with me now is I am worked to death and feel good for nothing. Out of eight monitors we have only four here on duty. They are getting used up in boiler and machinery and have to be continually repairing. Two have to be on picket duty at a time and when on this duty, there is not rest night or day. The Captain has to be up and awake all the time – exposed to the weather. The two days and nights off can scarcely be called off as we are only a short distance below the pickets and have to be on the alert for rams, torpedoes, blockade runners, t.(etc.) If I could only get off from this infernal duty, I would thank my stars. If without compromiseing me, you can get me relieved, I would consider it a lasting favour. I'm afraid my health will not stand it long. I have seen too much hard service to be in good condition to undergo so much fatigue and confinement.

I wonder if we could not get up some new kind of shell to explode under water to clear out obstructions and torpedoes in advance of vessels. Think of it. If we attempt to go in here, more than our Monitor will go down. There is no place inside here where we can get out of the fire of one hundred guns. Or out of narrow channels filled with obstruction and torpedoes. Three rebel deserters came in today with information that three hundred torpedoes had been put down within the last few days. My impression is that if public opinion forces us to go in, little or nothing will be accomplished, and if we get out with enough to keep the rebel scoundrels in check and prevent the blockade being raised and the troops driven off of Morris Island. In the mean time we will have left two of four Monitors sunk inside for the rebs to raise and use against us. So don't speak of this as coming from me. I hope that you will soon have a chance to build one of your vessels. I hope to see it afloat. And if we could only have a peace honorable to both parties without bloodshed among ourselves, what I greatly fear.

Write soon, if only a few lines – remember us kindly to Jenkins.

J. T. Curry

P.S. We have heard things from rebel sources of the nomination of McClellan or the platform union with constitutional right guaranteed or a vigorous prosecution of the war – if this is so, I think his election is sure. Don't mention what I said about our weakness of our force here.

Well, this did not sound like the grog and hornpipe version of seafaring that would induce a sane man to serve, but Nachron assured me that I would be spared any chance of engagement with an enemy. He reiterated an explicit promise that he would remove me at the threat of mortal danger, and since my trust in him was growing daily, I somewhat hesitantly agreed to his plan.

By sunset, I had given all the energy I cared to expend to getting myself ready for naval service. What kind of preparation would have enabled me to foresee the inconveniences of life among lepers in Central America or Nazis in New Mexico? What could possibly be next; volcanoes, dragons? If I could get a good night's sleep so my mental and physical reflexes would function optimally, I hoped I could trust luck and Nachron to do the rest. We had agreed that I would depart sometime during the following morning, but we felt that if I didn't know precisely when, the transition might be accomplished with less discomfort.

Mike Corbett

U.S.S. Sangamon, later renamed Jason

U.S. Naval Historical Center Photograph

"Twenty years from now you will be more disappointed by the things you didn't do than by the ones you did do. So throw off the bowlines, sail away from the safe harbor. Catch the trade winds in your sails. Explore. Dream. Discover."   Mark Twain

TWENTY

The Boat

"Here am I sitting in a tin can." I am driven nearly to distraction by the unwanted repetition of that David Bowie lyric in my mind. Although Major Tom had to cope with the infinity of space, I had merely to execute my modest duties as a crewman aboard a Union naval vessel patrolling a small piece of the U.S. Atlantic coastline. How I came to be here was thanks to a bit more of Mr. Nachron's wizardry. I was given the uniform and documentation in my own name that allowed me to replace a young seaman whose screaming nightmares made life for the rest of the crew impossible.

The War Between the States provided the raw material for lots of nightmares. Those veterans lucky enough to survive an infantry clash supported by cannon fire gave journalists and historians the vapors as they heard the explicit horrors of this war. As the haze that accumulated from thousands of tramping feet on dry ground rose to meet the smoky pall that accompanies gunfire, visual recollections gave way to auditory ones. The pfftt and buzz of bullets in flight, the thumping sound a larger bore round makes as it stops in mid-flight, and the grunts and screams through the miasmic confusion showed generations of Americans that even triumph may not have much glory in it.

Given the choice between charging up a hillside to dislodge its defenders with a primitive and undependable weapon, and joining the Union Navy, which due to the small size of the Confederate fleet, minimized the chance of lethal confrontation; it's shiver me timbers and break out the hardtack for me, matey.

When I first looked at the U. S. S. Sangamon, I wondered if my consent to continue this hare-brained odyssey might have been hasty. The craft, and that must be the most liberal use of the term, bore resemblance to no other design with the possible exception of a sunken railroad car, and since I was not presently curious about sea bottom exploration, I was unimpressed with my prospects. Here before me was the instrument for testing all the phobias I could think of except fear of heights.

Since my immune system was from an evolutionary standpoint, tuned to cope with stressors of twentieth century origin, I was fearful that I might be stepping on to a virtual Petri dish of opportunistic life forms. I shrugged away a spasm of contempt and prepared myself for a prolonged period of shallow breathing.

Those first introductory moments prior to boarding Sangamon would have driven a sane man to desert, but I naively persisted, so there I was. Before I relate my particular litany of complaints, it might be informative to describe U.S.S. Sangamon more thoroughly, since she, not the Civil War, constituted the specific framework of my dilemma.

If your only expectation of a boat* is to float freight downstream, then a simple design will suffice. Since stability and buoyancy can be achieved with a raft or a barge, complications and expense can be minimized. When it must serve more specialized purposes such as wartime might demand, potential problems multiply. My temporary home for the unknown but hopefully brief future was engineered to resist all but the most robust enemy fire, and its vulnerability was further minimized by its low profile and placement of key components beneath the water line. The handicaps of this exclusively military configuration were numerous however, and two stood out: 1) In order to keep so much of the boat under the water line, buoyancy had to be compromised. 2) Any sailor will tell you that due to the various deforming pressures on the hull, seams joining segments of wood or iron will leak. She was a sturdy pile of barely floating metal in precarious equilibrium between service as a temporary residence for 59 men and as a home for crabs.

As the most junior member of the crew, I was shown to a tiny compartment in the bow that was

---

* U.S.S. Sangamon was an 1875 ton Passaic-class monitor, but everybody who served aboard called her a boat.

not only a rope locker, but the sleeping quarters for a peculiar-smelling sailor named Satchel and myself. If it weren't the middle of the nineteenth century, I would swear my suite-mate was a glue sniffer, as his lethal aura was frequently accompanied by signs of chemical intoxication. Maybe he discovered something he liked while scraping paint or cleaning the twin vibrating lever engines, but I did not judge him too harshly, since I had no claim to innocence when it came to self-abuse.

Living in the pointy end of a boat, although uncomfortable, had some advantages. The location allowed me some degree of privacy as well as a distance from the noise of the engines and the occasional good-natured yawping of my fellow sailors. The real bonus though, was a narrow hatch through which I could squirm onto the deck and bathe daily. There was hot water enough for a weekly bath for every crew member, but my nose told me that few of my shipmates were attentive to that schedule. In fact, the general reek of sweating fungal human flesh frequently forced me to bury my face in the comforting dampness of the pile of oily ropes in my cabin.

There was really only one sailor that stood out from the others, olfactorily speaking. No morgue or landfill could compete with this guy's ability to inspire universal revulsion. I learned a lot about human behavior from him. For instance, when confronted by a noxious odor, almost no one pinches his nostrils together between thumb and index finger. That is more likely a gesture of contempt or derision. Most people, in the presence of inescapable fetor, will twitch uncomfortably for a second or two, look up, down, and sideways then try to pull their collars or sleeves over their faces so they can inhale through their own foulness. Mess (the perfect word) was frequently spirited off to various locations in order to avoid the inevitable sensory confusion that too many nauseating smells will produce. One of my fellow sailors almost burned his nose off by trying to use a lit candle as a kind of gas mask.

To this hygiene-deprived environment, add pervasive, uncontrollable dampness, which whether in the daytime heat or the chill of evenings would doubtlessly promote the growth of every organism smaller than a louse. We enjoyed the company of a few dozen rats as well, but they seemed to find plenty to eat without nibbling on our toes while we slept. It wasn't all misery. The guys were generally helpful and good-natured, and Captain Curry distributed the duties and rewards of shipboard life fairly.

One sailor in particular was quick to befriend me. He showed me the ropes, so to speak, and even offered a few congratulatory words about my enthusiasm for cleanliness. He was so curious about the smell of my twenty-first century soap, I believe he would have traded a week's ration of biscuits for it. We had many things in common, and although a few years my junior, he had a lively wit and an engaging smile. He said his name was Dan, and without his help, the length of my stay on the Sangamon might have doubled or tripled. It was my good fortune that at some point, Dan came up with the idea of swapping bunkmates, which Satchel passively agreed to since he would go almost anywhere he was aimed. Dan's bunk was in large common quarters and virtually no one even noticed the replacement, so the switch was made without fanfare.

Mr. Nachron's request was to retrieve an object that the skipper believed would be useful to the Navy, so Dan and I frequently speculated on the origin of an intermittent pinging noise that he believed was made by Captain Curry conducting some kind of test on the hull. When we were spared the throbbing of the engines and the random shipboard clatter of daily life, we could detect his rhythmic and exploratory plinking from different parts of the boat.

From what Dan and I were able to deduce, Curry believed that by tapping on any part of the hull thin enough to produce a ringing tone, he might learn something about the exterior. The device he had ingeniously made, which I had not yet seen, consisted of a small brass cup with a few dozen grains of gunpowder covered by the crystal from a pocket watch. His hope was that the gunpowder would jiggle differently if we were near another vessel or the sea bottom when he struck the hull sharply. Of course the likelihood that this could ever be of practical use was nil, but the principle will seem familiar to anyone acquainted with modern sonar. From his letters I knew the skipper was something of an inventor, and when he had completed his shipboard duties, you could sometimes hear him in his tiny cabin tinkering.

This and other subjects kept Dan and me awake long after all but the late watch had retired, and since the lengths of our missions were relatively short (the Sangamon was on patrol to detect blockade runners whose intent was to resupply the Confederate forces), we were speculating on how we might spend a twenty-four hour shore leave. During one of these nocturnal exchanges, there must have been a minor jolt from a wave, because Dan's foot seemed to fumble against my leg. Since our feet naturally drew close together at the bow anyway, this event was not in itself notable, but there is a threshold of time over which most gentlemen will become uncomfortable with skin against skin.

    I conjured up images of Ancient Greece, prisons, bathhouses, and prolonged isolation from the opposite sex. I assumed there was some protocol for dealing with invitations of this nature, (as in airport restrooms) but consent was the furthest option from my mind, so I smiled queasily and retreated from his touch. Dan's peculiar reaction was to grin broadly and emit a rather unmanly giggle. As he began to pull the shirt from one of his shoulders, I started coiling my body to spring through the hatch, since I had no intention of participating in any kind of frolic that did not involve pudenda.

    A moment before I could push the hatch open, I happened to glance behind me at Dan's soft white shoulder and part of a shapely breast. A what!! I had read of women successfully masquerading as men to enlist, but living aboard an armed vessel with its intimacy and inconvenience; I would not have thought it possible. As I slipped back within, Dan (actually Mary as I was to learn), unraveled her long history of poverty, withdrawal, abandonment, desperation, etc., etc., eventually resulting in our present situation. I was tempted to share information about the twenty-first century, with its attendant perils such as drugs, violence, and HIV, so she could see that her choices weren't so crazy, but I thought better of it. She might have been amused to learn of the future popularity of cross-dressing, even outside the theater.

As she tantalizingly continued to disrobe, I noticed what I should have seen all along. Her neck, waist, and legs were long with smallish feet and a general grace of movement that quickened my pulse. Don't judge me too harshly for my lascivious enthusiasm, since it had seemed like a hundred years since I had touched a woman, and I began to tremble for want of her. She placed her hand firmly on my chest, swore me to absolute secrecy about all of our confidences, and then pulled me gently into her arms. At first, I clung as a lichen, unmoving and rigid, but she slowly drew me into a swaying pelvic motion that became the first tiny whisper of the thunder that was to follow. We coupled so energetically that even in the frenzy of the most contorted positions, we were able to anticipate our nearly canine yelping and snarling, and smother most of them with hands or ropes.

Since insatiable passion is impossible to completely repress, particularly within a metal container, some of our crewmates had to have heard our thrashing. Fortunately for us, it must have sounded like combat except for its duration. What fistfight lasts for six hours? At any rate, the many bruises we both bore the next day in some way corroborated the fight theory and nothing more was made of the incident.

I spent the next day topside polishing various oddly named nautical doodads like binnacles and scuppers, a task that cannot possibly be accomplished without daydreaming, and I had plenty to dream about. Images of Dan/Mary came to me unbidden, and her scent remained on my body so pleasantly that I chose not to wash early that day. Oddly though, as I recalled my adventure from the night before, I could not dismiss the image of Marta's beautiful face poised above me in the candlelight. I was marveling at the strength, balance, and overall mastery of her body that enabled us to take such pleasure from physical nearness. How do you learn that in solitude? Was I really cultivating a dose of jealousy over a beautiful leper's perceived prior experience in the twentieth century while I prepared for another night with a cross-dressing nineteenth century sailor? Fortunately, I have the attention span of a brine shrimp and almost no capacity for self-scrutiny, so I survived the moment.

Something happened later that afternoon that accelerated my schedule. We drifted so close to the Carolina coast that I could smell hearth fires and southern cooking on the westering breeze, and I knew if I had to, I could swim easily to shore. I more or less trusted Mr. Nachron's solemn promise to extricate me from the Civil War once I had procured the object, but the contingency plan I had quickly formulated made me feel better about the whole enterprise. I had stupidly ignored the possibility that after my swim, I might be treated to the hospitality of a Confederate prison like Andersonville, with no cover story to discourage my potential captors from treating me as a spy.

I waited patiently for the skipper to take his evening meal with a few of the officers, and then crept stealthily into his unlocked quarters, where it didn't take too long to locate the little brass article that Nachron coveted since the Captain's possessions were pitifully few. Other than the expected pile of diagrams, orders, books, and personal correspondence, Curry had only a modest number of personal effects, and I located my prize in a short time.

Preoccupation with my search must have distracted me from awareness of footsteps approaching, since upon exiting the Captain's quarters, I ran right into Curry and one of his fellow officers. Before they could react, I charged headlong through the length of the vessel, knocking surprised crewmen aside in my flight. I pitched forward into my quarters where Dan/Mary was busy patching a pants leg or something, kissed her hard on the mouth while her stunned eyes opened widely, and bolted through the hatch. As the sounds of pursuit grew louder, I quickly surveyed the coastline and slipped overboard.

By then, it was almost dark enough to prevent the growing number of crew members on the deck of the Sangamon from seeing more than a few yards, but I swam underwater until my breath gave out to provide an extra margin of safety. Once I thought myself safely away from the boat, I broke the surface to refill my lungs, but just before I did, I thought I saw the shadowy profile of the monitor in front of me. Had I gotten turned around while underwater?

I thrust myself upward by kicking to the top of a swell and looked backwards to reassure myself of the Sangamon's location. Then I glanced ahead toward the shoreline, where to my horror, I caught sight of two tremendous sharks. My panic prevented me from weighing the respective merits of answering to military justice as opposed to trying to outswim two of nature's most efficient predators. Instead, as I raced back to the boat, I wondered if being torn apart by two sharks might be a more merciful death than swimming directly into the jaws of one, and surviving long enough to drown as it tried to choke me down. My speculation was interrupted by a familiar roar, the odd strobing light and then....

Mike Corbett

TWENTY-ONE

You can't swim on a wet carpet. I know this because I flopped around on Nachron's floor for long enough to fully realize I was out of harm's way with all my extremities intact.

"How fortunate that you were able to take time away from your shipboard duties to enjoy a refreshing swim," he quipped.

I slapped a puddle of 150 year old seawater that had accumulated on the rug, deliberately splashing my witty little friend. He hopped backwards like a wet kitten and sputtered momentarily before he regained his composure, then shockingly he began to laugh. He really did have a sense of humor, and I liked and trusted him more for it.

Over the next few hours, I gave him Captain Curry's gadget (in place of which I left all my coins) and related the details of my memorable nautical assignment. It was of no particular importance that I included the extra brass coin from Palo Seco along with the gold pieces in my pocket. I'm sure Curry would put it to use as a gasket or something and Nachron agreed. I omitted the juicy romantic segments of the tale, since I did not welcome his curiosity about my personal life any more than I needed his approval. However, his intuition or whatever star he followed, led him to fathom the entirety of my exploits. He understood, probably better than anyone on earth the value of being "in the moment", and my limitless capacity for instinctive responses reassured him that he had chosen well.

After a well-earned rest, I thought perhaps Crystal might be wondering about my absence, so I had a light meal and set out for a meeting with a couple of margaritas. I was pretty sure that my friend hadn't heard any lies as interesting as the truth I could have related, but I was afraid she wouldn't serve me if she thought I was already inebriated. Between taking care of the other customers, she provided me with the local gossip about which waitress was pregnant again and who got caught driving under the influence, but I was only half listening. My expectations of life in general and myself in particular had evolved, and I wanted to escape the self-imposed burden of my past habits and lunge blindly forward on another mission. Except for the painful memory of Lynn, I could have stepped into almost any new life but my own without hesitation.

Three margaritas later, I fell into the welcoming arms of a familiar stupor, and to Crystal I indicated my intention to buy a girl sitting nearby a drink. She posed provocatively on a bar stool with an overturned shot glass next to her cocktail and a

Mr. Nachron's List

partial pack of cigarettes atop a full one, so I surmised that she was no stranger to clubs. These factors, along with the suggestive tattoo on her hand and the uninhibited stare of a person who has no fear of being noticed, made me want to see what made her tick.

When I got Crystal's attention, she gave me an intense warning stare and drew her index finger across her throat. In barspeak, that means beware. No. Beware! And Crystal, with her broad range of experiences, would have no incentive to mislead me. Or would she? Maybe my old friend was a bit jealous and didn't want to share me. We had impulsively hooked up a few times in the past, and perhaps those memories inspired protectiveness, so as any drunken idiot would have done, I ignored her judgment and insisted on a cocktail for my new friend, who smiled the way a rattlesnake would if it could feel gratitude.

I endured fifteen minutes of a one-sided conversation about rehab and her boyfriend's unfair prison sentence before I began to contrive a diplomatic withdrawal. Crystal stood smirking with her arms crossed, and I was making a mental note never again to discount her advice when I felt a hand on my leg. As I stood up and excused myself to make a phone call, she blurted in a voice that could be heard above the loud music; "So you think you're too good for me too", and threw her unfinished drink at me. I fled for the relative safety of the men's room. From there, I could hear the commotion the bouncer, the girl, and a policeman who was called from the exterior made as the three of them tumbled onto the sidewalk amid her shrieks and the curses of her captors. She was unable to get the knife out of her tight denims before the handcuffs went on however, so no serious harm was done.

    This prickly episode made me reevaluate the life I had come from, and the one I was being drawn into, so with this in mind, I apologized to Crystal and returned to my temporary residence at chez Nachron. Due to the lateness of the hour, I quietly opened the door to find my host poring over some little object with a ten power magnifier. I begged his pardon for the interruption, but he graciously halted his effort to ask me if he could be of service.

    "Mr. Nachron; I mean Albert," I quickly corrected myself, "I feel so much more aware of not only the past, or the other 'now' that you patiently explained to me, I have an itch to know something about the future. You don't have to be specific, but if it's within your capabilities, just give me a little taste."

    "Ron," he began "I may be able to share a few observations with you, but I can't guarantee that the information won't be a bit depressing."

    I nodded stoically, and I think he knew he wouldn't alarm me, so he continued. "America will undergo many dramatic changes in the next century and not all of them will be productive. There is already a growing tendency to replace achievement with a sense of entitlement. This transition will be accompanied by an accelerating inability to educate our children, who will perhaps as a consequence, proceed down their inevitable path toward life-threatening obesity. Have you noticed the commercial trend toward supersizing? Madison Avenue is busily tailoring our preferences to conform to more liberal standards. All the news isn't bad, however. The medical and scientific communities of India and China are already working on a process to insulate the vital organs against the deleterious effects of excessive adiposis. With the export of this technique to the great consuming nations, it may be possible for their populations to live long and fruitful lives with only a slight sacrifice of mobility, since everyone will have his own personalized vehicle that can transport one thousand pounds at thirty miles an hour."

Well I was pretty sure I wouldn't need to ask questions like that any more unless I had consumed enough alcohol to forget what I heard when I woke up, so I made a mental note to pay my dues at the gym and start eating more roughage.

Mike Corbett

TWENTY-TWO

"Good morning Ron."

I didn't see him come in the room, and I never heard him unless he was rooting around his treasures, but here he was, smiling as if we were just normal people in an everyday world. The particular expression he wore, as I had periodically observed, was introductory to his offering me yet another so-called travel opportunity.

"The difference," he said, "is that you will be revisiting your own past, and although circumstances may seem slightly altered, certain persons and places may be quite familiar. I expect you will want to thank me for this chance to double back on your own joyful youth. There will be no charade, no danger to speak of, and although you will never be recognized for it, you may be the instrument for saving lives. All that I require of you is that you take a little trip to a tropical paradise and bring back a fish that is destined for extinction.

The fish need not survive since it is the parasite within that fish that is of interest to me. If you consent to perform this errand, I will provide you with the wherewithal to purchase the necessary equipment, including a cooler to keep the fish at the perfect temperature until you return. This is a unique chance for both of us to accomplish something praiseworthy, so I hope your cooperation will begin apace."

We both knew I couldn't resist this one. I was being given the opportunity to go to a place of nearly pristine natural beauty and do a little fishing, which was my favorite pastime in those formative years. How could I refuse?

Preparation for this outing would be relatively simple since there was plenty of appropriately dated currency still available if you took the time to locate it, and every obstacle I could anticipate might be overcome with a fistful of cash. To my surprise, Nachron proposed that I also bring a small sealed bag of a substance that looked like marijuana. I couldn't imagine why he felt the need to supply me with a recreational drug, or why he thought it wouldn't be simple for me to acquire it on my own, but he insisted that the potency of his little package far exceeded that of anything I could have found, and therefore suited our purposes. As unusual as this sounded, Nachron's suggestions had proven quite useful so far, so I shrugged my shoulders and went downstairs to see if I could find a fishing magazine to entertain me until my departure.

I had only to wait until the next morning, since thanks to a discussion with my host, it seemed increasingly likely that I could be sent across the years without the shock and loss of equilibrium if I remained unconscious. Due to my elevated level of preparation for an abrupt appearance in a strange place, I slept soundly and woke up in a beachfront hotel about three miles from Nachron's apartment.

"Those who do not remember the past are condemned to repeat it." George Santayana

TWENTY-THREE

Flamingo

It wasn't hard to find Brownie again. His real name was Horatio, but most of our classmates just called him by his last name after exhausting the sophomoric possibilities his first name offered. He still lived a few blocks from Cardinal Gibbons High School in northeast Fort Lauderdale, where most of our fishing and surfing trips originated. Since deriving the most pleasure from either sport requires the appropriate conditions, like a northeast wind for instance, our attendance record suffered during certain seasons. All I had to do was persuade my old pal to turn his pool skimming duties over to one of his co-workers so we could spend some time stalking the wily moonfish, and I knew Nachron's incentive package would be an irresistible inducement if reliving the good times with an old buddy weren't enough.

    We filled up his pickup with gas and got on the turnpike heading south before the daily inconvenience of rush hour traffic. Our destination was the southern tip of the peninsula, specifically a lodge and marina called Flamingo, located within a national park. With any luck, we wouldn't need the small boat we trailered for the sake of versatility, since it seemed our quarry might be reasonably plentiful under the dock within the small harbor. I was anxious to complete the task at hand, but there were a few obstacles I had anticipated and one I had not.

    Although the Florida Keys have been claimed and sanitized to some extent by civilization, most of Everglades National Park's vast area has not overly suffered from human contamination. An increase in water temperature and a slight decrease in purity and salinity as well as the introduction of a few non-native species can be traced back to man's heavy hand, but for the most part it is nature's empire, not ours. If you don't believe me, just stand outside for a few hours in any warm month, and when you collapse from the weight of the engorged mosquitoes, you may get close enough to the ground to notice the opportunistic flora that seem to be assembling around you to gain some foothold on anything the insects might have left behind.

    It is within such places that populations of mammals, insects, reptiles and fish can thrive for perhaps a few more decades before the unfortunate but inevitable trajectory of extinctions becomes a popular cause.

Our specific objective was the moonfish or lookdown as it is sometimes called, having the general appearance of an anorexic pompano with a redesigned head sloping down to a tiny mouth. I had never seen a moonfish at Flamingo, but that may have been because of the increased number of mosquitoes in the evening hours and the nocturnal feeding preferences of both species. I was told that this single population of fish had a slightly different caudal configuration and larger than normal eyes. And only this particular creature, according to Nachron, could be host to the parasite he required for his obscure purposes.

We got a room at the small lodge and planned our first evening around the setting of the sun, when the lights would come on to provide the most desirable environment for moonfish to forage around the pilings and hunt for food. I staked out a likely segment of the dock between two small boats and bumped a tiny feathered jig up and down on the edge of the light, where I hoped the clear water wouldn't work against me. So far, nothing I wanted was curious about my artificial bait, but Brownie was sitting about thirty feet away in a cloud of sweet-smelling smoke (he had opened Nachron's package) and laughing wildly as he slapped the water with trout skins that a late-arriving angler had just discarded. Two eighty pound tarpon were competing to pull the skins from Brownie's hand, and he teased them the way you would ask a dog to beg. Few people know tarpon behave that way, being such sought-after game fish, but Flamingo was and is a special place.

Both tarpon and mosquitoes are members of ancient families that evolution has had no reason to change, and at that moment Brownie and I had the full attention of both. I sprawled across the dock on my stomach with my head and arms over the edge in the time-honored fashion of the dedicated pier fisherman. Not only was half of my body inaccessible to the humming horde of blood suckers, but from my excellent vantage point I could drop my lure into the perfect spot to deceive my prey. Incidentally, if you thought mosquitoes could be discouraged by the application of a few layers of repellent, you are obviously unfamiliar with the wildest Florida variety. A Fort Lauderdale mosquito will hover and land lightly on some exposed area to test its scent or tenderness. The Everglades variety simply flies into anything that moves, proboscis extended, and penetrates with a tiny thump. I was playing host to a few hundred of the latter type, which were in no way inconvenienced by the poisonous chemical coating I had applied an hour earlier.

After catching and releasing a small snook and a variety of other healthy juvenile fish, I thought I saw two of Nachron's would-be trophies curl around a piling. I dropped the jig into the darkness and bumped it into the approximate direction the moonfish were heading and within forty seconds, I had captured the silvery prize. My regret at allowing this creature to die by my hand would be tempered, Nachron promised, by the enormous benefits the parasite within could provide. With the elation that accompanies a tough job nearly completed, I jumped from the dock, yelled to Brownie that I had scored, and hightailed it for the lodge. This flurry of motion did not trouble the carpet of mosquitoes on my back since they were all by then too heavy to take flight. I had hoped my human companion was right behind me so he could beat them senseless with a towel, but he was nowhere to be found. In fact, that hour on the dock was the last time we would ever see each other.

    My intention was to place the moonfish as quickly as possible into an ice chest with some slightly cooled salt water in it that we had left strapped down in the little flats boat, then go hunting for my friend. I hoped the pot he smoked hadn't caused him to join the tarpon in their aquatic playground, but he was impulsive that way. The time I spent searching was just enough to permit something else to happen that I hadn't counted on, however, and it nearly scuttled my mission.

    Did you know raccoons cannot be stopped by twist-off caps, pop-tops or childproof containers? They can raid live bait wells, open potato chips or chew through heavy canvas if they sense a treat, and although they tend to share nuts and pretzels, they will fight like angry cats over a peanut butter and jelly sandwich.

    I walked to the front of the lodge just in time to see a tribe of the little masked thieves absconding with my moonfish. The alpha raccoon had it in his paws and teeth, so reckoning that he was in no position to effectively defend himself, I sprang at him. The filthy little rodent* was quicker than I thought, even toting a pound of rare fish, but I was gaining on him as he plunged into the moonless night.

We scrambled into a small open area surrounded by palmettos and overhung by large branches, where to my surprise, the little bandit turned to face me with the moonfish at his feet. He was standing nearly upright as if to challenge my right of ownership, but just as I thought to reclaim my prize, I noticed other eyes in the dark background, some large and unblinking, others in the branches, yellow and malicious. Had I been led into a trap? Alligators, snakes, and Florida panthers could not be conspiring with raccoons to catch a human using a fish as bait. It was preposterous. I would never know what might have happened, since as soon as I got my hands on the disputed property, I heard the strange noise and felt the sensation of being drawn back to Nachron's apartment.

---

* The raccoon is of course not a member of the order of Rodentia. Ron, in his frustration, was seeking a pejorative term.

TWENTY-FOUR

I stood in the living area, covered with sweat and insect bites that I could account for, and a set of well-spaced tooth marks on my lower leg that I could not. Without even a nod of welcome from my diminutive host, he snatched the fish from my hands and placed it in a pan full of liquid he had obviously prepared for that purpose. For him, apparently, it was mission accomplished and on to the next case. As for me, I felt there were some questions to be answered.

"What the hell is so darned important about that parasite that I had to risk my skin and kill a perfectly innocent fish?" I demanded.

He sat down, sighed, and began patiently to elaborate. "My boy, killing that fish was a regrettable necessity in order to retrieve the creatures living within it. They may one day be responsible for saving countless lives due to their unique ability to neutralize the effects of anthrax poisoning.

This particular parasite was destined for extinction, so if it can be reintroduced to a compatible species, there may be much to be grateful for. I have anticipated that a bit more of your boundless curiosity might be about the friend you recruited to help you."

Nachron was right. If Brownie had somehow come to harm because of my influence, the whole enterprise would be tarnished and my heroism would be called into question.

He continued. "Your friend ran afoul of some members of the local community by carelessly chatting up the underage daughter of a Cuban fisherman. His boldness, coupled with his obvious intoxication, for which I blame myself, resulted in his arrest by local officials and a trip to a Monroe County jail. He was able to get his boat, truck, and all of its contents back within forty-eight hours."

I had one last question, specifically about that bag of pot, and how that seemed like a hindrance at best.

He had a sympathetic expression on his face as he resumed. "Your friend had been diagnosed with an aggressive cancer a week prior to your arrival. It was my wish to mitigate the discomfort he was destined to endure for the next two months, after which no relief would be necessary."

As I sat in the bathtub I reflected on an old friendship, a new friendship, and the memory of the electrifying sensation of Lynn's hands on my now ravaged skin.

For the next two days, the afternoon sun and the warm water of the Atlantic Ocean brought me more relief than a team of doctors with unguents and lotions could have done. I would float sleepily in the shallows for an hour, and then walk south toward Port Everglades inlet until almost sundown.

Late in the second afternoon, I saw something so surprising that I thought I had been unknowingly transported again. Somehow Nachron, in a baggy red bathing suit, had located me. As he approached with his smooth shiny hairless pale skin (I think it was skin), he looked like some kind of round beach toy bumping along in the wind. In spite of his size, he was agile enough to match my stride as he attempted to engage me in conversation about his next project. However, since he was becoming short of breath, he proposed that we dine together to discuss the possibilities, and by the end of our walk that seemed like a pretty good idea.

We sat outside at Mango's Restaurant and finished a bottle of reasonable Cabernet and most of our meal without saying a word about our next collaboration. Although we reviewed some pleasant memories of adventures past, he suggested that perhaps we might lubricate the rest of the conversation with a bit of very old brandy in the privacy of his apartment, so I knew this time it was special.

Mike Corbett

TWENTY-FIVE

Transformation

I was no longer surprised by any of the conversations Nachron initiated, nor was I unaware that I was about to be persuaded to perform yet another errand. As we sat in his living room, he seemed a bit more serious about this proposal than he had been previously.

"Ron," he tentatively began, "although you have demonstrated extraordinary versatility by blending into the environments you have visited on my behalf, I fear my next objective may test even your considerable talents. A medical doctor who could speak fluent German would be ideal in the role I am considering. Do you think you could pull it off?"

Since I speak about twenty words of German and I suffer from a lifelong case of hypochondria, I replied "Ja, Herr Nachron, I am at your service."

I knew he wasn't joking, but I wasn't so sure about myself.

"Your enthusiasm is laudable," he continued, "but do not underestimate this challenge. Your success will depend on your ability to convince people that you are a seventeenth century man of medicine. For the sake of authenticity, it would be helpful if you brushed up on your German, but we may be able to pass you off as a Finn with limited language skills. You may presumably cobble your ideas together in French or English and perhaps seem a bit of an oddity, which may be to your advantage in the court of Leopold. Your medical dossier might be enhanced if we double your traveling supply of antibiotics and add a few pain killers to be used only in extreme situations."

As I considered this new dilemma, I thought I might make immediate use of a sedative to relieve some of my concerns regarding Nachron's outlandish new wish. Did he expect me to function believably in a time and culture that would be so alien and possibly hostile? Along with the obvious barriers of language and profession, I had to somehow counterfeit the demeanor of an aristocrat, and if you have read this far, you will rightfully assume that such an imposture would be against my nature. Since I had during my last missions been assured that no physical harm would befall me, it seemed I really had nothing to lose but my time, and I no longer had a grasp of the meaning of that four-letter word, so I could think of no reason to object.

In preparation for my visit to Habsburg Austria, I visited the Fort Lauderdale Public Library to brush up on the life I was about to be conducted into, but I did not need reference material to remind me that certain human qualities have remained unchanged over millennia. For example, beauty, wealth, and influence have always been at once beneficial and potentially dangerous. The only asset that does not inspire people to covet or resent is charm, which will often deliver where swagger fails. Any wisdom I possess from the twenty-first century would certainly produce anxiety if used willy-nilly in the seventeenth, thus making an increasingly strong argument for remaining as inconspicuous as possible for the duration, and even with tight pants and powdered hair, I believed I could escape notice. I was nearly correct in this assumption.

My research into the seventeenth century world of European culture revealed a confusion of tactical efforts on the part of the Austrians, Germans, Spanish, French, Ottomans and others to expand their influence by war, marriage, and intrigue. I was to appear in the court of Leopold I, sometimes called "The Hogmouth" due to an unfortunate genetic trait that had survived admirably thanks to incautious breeding. Once introduced, along with many others in attendance, I was expected to eat, drink, and converse with no particular function other than as an ornament. Once again, I thought to congratulate Nachron on his assessment of my potential.

In order to conform to the stylish demands of Leopold's court, Nachron and I had to backdate my wardrobe somewhat. We purchased enough silk and phony jewels to outfit a Key West parade, and although this may have seemed odd to a small town haberdasher, Fort Lauderdale's trendy costumers didn't bat an eye. Granted, it may have been supposed that we were the property managers of a troupe of thespians, but we were perceived by most shop owners as an odd little older man and his fancy caged bird. Nachron was mercifully insensitive to the pointing and whispering that accompanied our shopping trips, but I had the nagging fear that my sexual orientation might require a bit of clarification in the future.

During one of the many visits the tailor made to alter my growing wardrobe, Crystal walked unannounced into Nachron's apartment. I had never actually seen her laugh heartily. She was a gifted smirker and at times a subdued chuckler, but never to my knowledge, a victim of uncontrollable mirth. She scared us a little by falling down in such a paroxysm of violent laughter that her face turned bright red and her eyes filled with tears. She mumbled something vulgar about peacocks, but I couldn't make it out through the guffaws. I thought she tarnished the delicacy of the fairer sex with such an unladylike outburst, but I caught Nachron suppressing a giggle too, so I may have underestimated my ability to amuse.

My familiarity with seventeenth century habits, thanks to Nachron's coaching, broadened significantly in the next 48 hours. I learned how to turn from the hips, prance like a purebred pony, and behave with great condescension to the serving folks. I promised to keep my trap shut when someone dressed fancier than I deigned to speak, and if I had an inclination to object or contradict, I was instructed to merely nod wisely in agreement. If I could only understand the language, I believed

I had the raw material to become a somewhat convincing dandy. I was warming to the role, you see, but the litmus test for my performance would come when I was placed in country.

In the meantime, my dreams became more alarmingly vivid. Talking Lipizzaners and monarchs with crowned heads sat together at sumptuous tables with covered dishes served by gnomelike waiters. The bending of time and space had warped my imagination to conform to my adventures, and my identity was slowly but steadily blurring into the multiple backgrounds to which it was exposed.

I woke up in Vienna.

Leopold I, the "Hogmouth" as Acis in "La Galatea"

(1667, by Jan Thomas van Ieperen)

"Time flies on restless pinions – constant never."
Freidrich Schiller

TWENTY-SIX

Vienna

I was adjusting to the round trips from the twenty-first century quite comfortably. The remarkable phenomenon that Christian Doppler identified and the visual confusion that once accompanied my passage through the temporal barriers were no longer affecting my equilibrium, and other than a little initial drowsiness, I felt alert and quite normal in short order. The ease with which I casually violated accepted scientific principle seemed like a positive development, but I was to learn otherwise.

I had only been steady enough to consider my new surroundings for a few minutes, which consisted of a comfortable suite of rooms complete with a portrait of Leopold himself, when I heard a polite rapping at the door. I was informed in a prissy French voice that I was expected in the summer chamber in one hour. With the help of Nachron's prompting, I had memorized the sequence of dress and behavior that were to accompany the peculiar ceremonies of court life. For example, I was advised to avoid obvious inebriation during daylight hours, which turned out to be quite easy since the dreadful array of Austrian beverages, particularly the deceptively named wines, were repulsive enough to sicken long before they intoxicated.

The summer chamber was so named because of its seasonal exposure to a barrage of seventeenth century sunlight with almost no pollution to deflect it. The tall windows permitted an unobstructed view of the magnificent geometric gardens and the mountains beyond, and those whose job was to tend the foliage were instructed to traverse the grounds only along the measured lines of flora. If a gardener inadvertently wandered diagonally across an open area, he might be exiled to the Bohemian Erzgebirge to mine silver for the Empire.

Except for the group of lively attractive women around a gaming table, the afternoon gathering was a quiet affair. Subdued conversation and the detailed comparisons of an amazing number of Viennese pastries made me not care if I spoke German or not. My presence was not noted by any of the occupants of the grand room, so I edged casually toward the animated group of stunners who seemed to be enjoying themselves gambling at backgammon. That ancient game was among many that I had learned to play competitively during my largely misspent youth, so I leaned forward to kibitz.

To my amazement, one of the girls had embarked on a strategy that I would have sworn was the exclusive property of a more recent century. By introducing a large number of checkers to her opponent's home board, she was creating a series of obstacles through which safe passage was nearly impossible. The unwary victim was clucking happily at her prospects, unable to sense the peril that awaited her several rolls of the dice later. When the gloating halfwit began to lose multiple pieces to her clever opponent and finally see them hopelessly trapped behind my new heroine's wall of six consecutive points, she pouted and threw a small purse of shiny gold coins on the table so hard that some scattered to the floor.

The loser's pretty face turned ugly as she glared at the onlookers who were gaily applauding the successful gambit and its architect, but I was a model of restraint. The beautiful game master's eyes found me easily since I was the only viewer who wasn't whooping delightedly. She briefly smiled in my direction, glanced away, then looked back and did something I could never make anyone else believe. Under the admiring eyes of at least twenty people, she slyly stared directly into my eyes and pushed her tongue firmly against the interior of her cheek, causing it to distend most provocatively.

I looked up to see the reactions of the others to this flattering gesture, but no eyes seemed to have caught it. I briefly considered the likely anachronism of what I felt must be a more contemporary signal to arouse a gentleman's nether region, but I quickly began to doubt my memory of what had happened. Perhaps there was some crusty archduke standing behind me for whom the flirtation was intended. In any event, by the time my composure had returned, she was chittering merrily with her gaming friends, leaving me to speculate on how many other games she might have mastered.

As I left that interesting bevy of celebrants, I was stopped by a plumpish dowager who politely addressed me in French. She had been told, I supposed, that my cultural limitations prevented me from communicating with many of the other guests. She pressed her advantage and informed me that I had become something of a curiosity at the Court of Leopold since I was fully three inches taller than anyone else I encountered during my visit. There was one fairly tall woman named Claudia whom I took to be of royal birth by virtue of her enormous underslung jaw and protruding lips.

The Habsburg genes were not distributed widely enough to give evolution a fair chance, but what might seem a deformity in the twenty-first century was a symbol of family pride in the seventeenth. There were dozens of people strutting proudly around the Imperial estate with vaguely porcine features, and a great many others who made themselves up that way as an homage. The tall girl needed no makeup however, as I was able to determine during a playful evening in which we danced cheek to snout and drank champagne (imported).

The dowager who admired my stature was named Anatole, and thanks to her wide knowledge of the personalities and habits of those who surrounded her, I learned that Leopold was about to take his third wife, and other than winning a war or suppressing an indigenous population, no event pleased the gentry more than another Imperial wedding. The lucky bride-to-be was none other than the brazen little strategist that I had admired a short time earlier. She herself was a Newburgian Princess, and by coincidence, the owner of an item that Nachron coveted more than any other.

Elle, the nickname the princess later insisted I use, was the owner of a tiny silk purse of unknown origin. It was so cleverly or perhaps magically created as to conceal the secrets of its construction, even under extreme magnification. It felt more like liquid glass than silk, and there was no good name for its color, since that changed according to the light it was exposed to. The real mystery of the purse, however, was how to open it. Although it was slightly less than two inches square, it obviously had an interior pocket, but no amount of investigation or coaxing yielded its secret. I later learned that although a strong man could not have torn it apart, if he placed it on his palm and blew lightly on it, it would fall open as if by magic to reveal its contents. Unknown to Nachron, and for the most part to me, the only thing that the purse had ever contained was a bright, nearly perfect diamond of well over two carats.

It was through Anatole's intercession that Elle and I became friendly enough to stroll around the gardens and play backgammon nightly. Leopold was busy planning invasions, treaties, and means by which to expand the Imperial treasury, so he had little time to spend with the future mother of an emperor. I never thought of backgammon as an aphrodisiac, but during our long sessions, in which I shared some very useful tricks of the game with her, Elle would remove a tiny shoe and stroke the interior of my calf, then my thigh, with her talented toes.

    Anatole would occasionally join us to share the day's whispered gossip. For her benefit we spoke French, but if Elle was feeling naughty, which was more often than not the case, she used English, in which she was quite fluent. I had assumed that Anatole was totally ignorant of that language, but one evening Elle playfully uttered something like "I want to taste the skin on your index finger", and she giggled uncontrollably, so maybe I was mistaken. If it seemed that a romance was budding that had the potential to disrupt the whole empire, it was not so. Elle was merely playing a game.

    Although her imagination and versatility were admirable, she never looked at me as a candidate for any but her carnal interests. I sensed that the sexual table she was preparing had some promised delicacies that grew in number and variety daily, but we had never even approached the threshold of actual physical intimacy. When that moment finally arrived, the passion that had grown so quickly between us was accompanied by answers to questions I had thus far failed to ask.

    The revelations which Elle shared with me on that first night that we found ourselves fumbling to remove each other's clothing made me glad I was a doctor. She confessed that she had made a few unwise choices during a period of youthful sexual experimentation, and the consequence of one of them was a bit of physical discomfort that she couldn't seem to shed. Luckily, I had enough of a powerful antibiotic in my luggage to restore pelvic health to an entire squad of Texas high school cheerleaders, so I was glad for both of us.

Secondly, and more challenging, the amazing purse with the diamond inside had somehow gotten lost in her ductwork, if you catch my meaning.

Why she chose to hide her treasure in such an intimate location I cannot guess, but my effort to help her regain her health and property required a great deal of patience and ingenuity. You may correctly assume that I was in some small way responsible for the extension of the Imperial line, but modesty inclines me to avoid satisfying the prurient taste for detail.

Under normal circumstances, which these did not resemble, Elle and I might have been aware that our "friendship" would eventually raise suspicious eyebrows, but our project was so mutually absorbing that we took no note of the conspiracy of whispers that would lead to our exposure. It may have been Anatole's penchant for disseminating juicy gossip, or it could have been Claudia, the tall dancer whose interest in displacing Elle as Empress may have been jealous or proprietary, but in either case our friendship had gained sufficient notoriety to doom it.

During the times that Elle was inaccessible due to her calendar of formal social obligations, I was left to my own diversions. When I wearied of the pomp and frippery at the palace, I would take long walks into what was then, and is today, a magnificent city. I got a genuine sense of the popularity of the Habsburgs not only from what I heard on the streets, but what I didn't hear. The generally positive outlook of the Viennese people implied that Leopold's empire satisfied its population in ways that even one of today's sophisticated democracies might have found challenging. There was an obviously prosperous merchant class, and although I never really mingled with the poorest tier of the population, I sensed a pervasive sense of well-being that was probably enhanced by the mild seasonal temperatures.

Since my life at court was increasingly designed by Elle's preference and availability, it may seem that I was the willingly expendable plaything of a selfish mistress. This was to some extent true, but although it must be said that romantic love had probably never occurred to milady with either Leopold or me, at least for my part the limitations were apparent. Given different circumstances and a lot more time, I might have learned to love her honestly and without reservation, but for the time being I was happy serving her in any way that gave her pleasure.

Don't feel too sorry for me. For a gentleman to be used and eventually dismissed by a lady is not without precedent. In fact, for centuries queens and empresses who required the odd distraction would flatter a suitable gentleman to serve her in ways that morally flexible religious leaders simply turned their backs to. Also, you may remember from a previous reference that I had some experience with being discarded that might help to minimize any emotional awkwardness.

After a particularly festive night in the palace, we found ourselves carelessly sprawled across a large cushion in Elle's quarters. We had placed a backgammon board between us with legs entangled, and the combined weight of our gossamer attire could not have exceeded three ounces. We had become so comfortable with our relationship by then that it prevented our anticipating the breach of our privacy by the suspicious Claudia. She had somehow found a key to Elle's locked quarters and boldly poked the majority of her long face into our recreation, and upon witnessing the entire vignette, she uttered some untranslatable insults at both of us and flew from the room threatening vengeance in Leopold's name. Elle took my hand in hers and told me she had nothing to fear because Leopold was so enamored of her and indifferent to the opinions of others, but she added that the same privileges may not be extended to me.

    I was reasonably certain that if I could get clear of the palace and into the crowded city, I could hunker down and wait for Nachron to extract me, so I quickly dressed. Elle stopped me at the door to press the little purse, about which I had completely forgotten, into my hand with the explanation that it was a small price to pay for a course of such tender and effective medical treatment. I smiled gratefully and reluctantly, because our mutual regard had become a strong bond, and then I fled into the hallway.

    Some kind of guard or servant in fancy gear was close enough to choose the heroic option of obstructing my escape, but he underestimated my determination. I turned, planted my right foot for balance, and sent a well-aimed left foot into his lower chest. He looked at me like I had violated one of the Marquis of Queensbury's rules, gasped, and then turned pink as he collapsed to the floor. As I hopped over his contracting form, I generously dropped one of my unused gold coins onto his chest to compensate him for the discomfort I had caused. I proceeded to jog down the long hallway until I saw something extremely frightening coming toward me, clearly intending to oppose me with lethal force.

If I had formed a negative impression of Claudia's preposterous face when we danced, enraged she was hideous. Like a monstrous fairy-tale avenger, she closed on me with a murderous sneer, competently brandishing a long blade. I made a right angle turn down another hallway where my friend Anatole, standing at the door to her chambers, signaled that I make a right turn down yet another hall. I nodded my appreciation and sprinted headlong toward an uncertain fate, but I still felt I could escape with a bit of luck.

Just as I thought I had put some distance between me and my pursuer, the slashing horror came around the corner with her sword high and foam flying from her absurd lips. Anatole was the instrument of this betrayal, and I wished I could inform Elle of her cruel trick, but there was hardly time for that. I reversed my direction once more and ran toward a growing number of normal looking humans who seemed unlikely to execute me on the spot for merely being a thorough physician. As I approached the relative safety of the startled crowd of courtiers and servants, I felt a nasty burning sensation from the nape of my neck to mid-thigh, but before I had time to identify its origin, I was once again looking up from the floor into Nachron's oddly worried eyes.

TWENTY-SEVEN

"Are you alright?" he asked as I attempted to once again peel myself from Nachron's carpet. "You gave me a bit of concern running back and forth in that hall my boy. Hard to get a fix on you, so to speak."

As I rose, I noticed that I had left a thin red stain about four feet long on the floor where I had recently arrived. He was mumbling about something as he skillfully attended my superficial wound, so I decided to lift his spirits by presenting him the purse he wanted so badly.

"Ron, you have gained my thanks and admiration for so deftly acting in such challenging circumstances, but obtaining this wonderful purse must be the final favor I ask of you. It is getting easier to send you off and increasingly more difficult to bring you back in a timely fashion, so your well-being, as evidenced by this little scratch on your back, may become impossible to guarantee. You may have the contents of the purse as a bonus for services rendered."

At the time, I expressed my profuse thanks for the stone, but if I had a notion of its market value, I would have dropped to my knees and groveled shamelessly. My disappointment at the cancellation of my adventure travel ticket was counterbalanced by the dream that a well-heeled and financially independent guy like me might be appealing to Lynn if, as Nachron assured me, we could locate her. I felt an unexpected twinge of sadness as I lay on the couch with a flipper on my chest scanning the mindless visual entertainments of the twenty-first century, so I decided to irritate Crystal by drinking myself into an amnesiacal stupor.

The short walk to Murray's Pub did nothing to discourage me from that goal, although it was interrupted by someone on a cell phone driving up over the curb and onto the sidewalk, narrowly avoiding the addition of more bloodstained clothing to my wardrobe. If South Florida does not lead the world in the vehicular slaughter of pedestrians and bicyclists, we are at least in contention for that distinction. Idiots routinely drive away from the carnage they create, hoping that they had merely slaughtered an undocumented immigrant, and praying that the delay would not make them too late for the early bird at Rotelli's.

Was I really missing my trips into the past, or had all the stress finally managed to crack my façade? In any case, Crystal and her many concoctions would be a welcome relief. Several hours later, she helped me through the door of her apartment and onto the sofa, where she

Mr. Nachron's List

threatened to beat the hangover off me if I puked on her furniture. She said I would probably blame her for serving me too many drinks, and in mid-sentence I started snoring. I woke up with a problem I had expected; a terrible headache, and one I had not; that I had forgotten where I put the diamond. Most people would have reacted to that realization with enough enthusiasm to launch an immediate search for the missing bauble, but I chose the easy option and fell back asleep for six more hours.

I was never materialistic to the exclusion of convenience, and apparently a few weeks of caroming around in a temporal maze hadn't altered my fundamental nature. The stone reappeared later that day in my underwear in that funny little compartment that nobody uses on the front of men's briefs. I had carelessly shoved the stone into the pocket of one of the many pairs of pants that Lynn had penetrated with her fingernail, and from there, it had somehow migrated into that aperture. Crystal later joked that the little stone had enjoyed more experience with genitalia than she had, but I wasn't sure whether laughter would be tasteless, so I just let it be.

Sleeping was no longer providing the relief and rejuvenation that I was so desperately in need of. For one thing, all this crazy travel had totally disrupted my circadian cycle, and I was learning to adjust to two hour periods of unconscious, followed by an hour of restless and disruptive thrashing.

Then there were the dreams. Initially, they ran like pleasant travelogues, but with the passage of time and events, they became more alarming and less realistic, or at least I hoped they did not reflect reality. I would sometimes see myself on a normal beach with the sun shining on a faceless female companion. Then the entire image would be captured by a gravitational force and begin to distort, bending the environment and the subjects slowly into amorphous shapes. At other times, in contrast to the increasingly distorted perspective of my visions, I was visited by those little pink triangles, but they were no longer benign. They swarmed and veered aggressively in my direction, as if to assure me that I was no longer part of their pantheon. I would wake up nauseated and worried that I might be learning to see reality the way it actually was, without the subjective bias of human interpretation.

Crystal, Nachron and I all agreed that the time had come for a long rest or a big change in my life. Eventually I decided on both. I would do the one thing that could change my life the most, which was to find Lynn. With the conclusion of that long pursuit, I could relax and learn to begin what I hoped would be a normal life. I knew it could never really be normal. I just needed a foothold like a clam to keep me from swirling away in some random eddy.

I should have guessed that Albert Nachron already had more than an inkling about what was to be. He stopped me on my way to a walk down the riverfront with news that he had located Lynn, and that she was in Central Florida. My breathing stopped for about ten seconds, after which I started making plans to leave the next morning.

TWENTY-EIGHT

Lynn

The trip from Fort Lauderdale to Winter Park shouldn't take more than about four hours. Crystal had two days off, so she agreed to keep me company if I would promise to get us a suite in a hotel with a good restaurant and spa, and since Nachron had made good on his promise to compensate me, I not only had a swollen bank account, I probably owned one of the finest three carat diamonds in existence. During the course of what is usually a pleasant and uneventful car trip, I had time to remember the remarkable period of my life in which I had subconsciously programmed myself to wake up just a little earlier than Lynn for the sheer ecstasy of watching her open her eyes in the morning. With that vision intruding on my effort to maintain control of the car, my hands literally trembled on the steering wheel in anticipation of seeing her again. I have been the beneficiary of a wealth of advantages: a dream to chase, unique experiences to savor, and the friendship of the sleeping woman beside me, whose simple expectations were that I be happy and not too boring.

When Nachron told me he had located Lynn, and furthermore that she was safe, accessible, and unattached, I pumped his hand and hugged him so hard I think he emitted a tiny squeaky fart. I thought we had so successfully satisfied his appetite for acquisition, that he might have shared my enthusiasm for a romantic reunion, but he was oddly subdued. His cryptic explanation for why I shouldn't get my hopes too high perplexed me. His exact words were: "My boy, Lynn essentially possesses all the amazing qualities you are so fond of, but she is more, much more than the person you remember. Her true nature is unknown to me, but I suspect she may be quite special indeed." Well I knew she was special all along, so I didn't attach sufficient importance to his counsel at the time.

Approaching central Florida from the south, you notice the gradual replacement of typical native flora with gas stations, motels, gift shops and the hundreds of other commercial enterprises that depend on the Magic Kingdom for their existence. There was a time when I might have appreciated the ingenuity that transformed native grasslands into forty-stall restrooms and underwater miniature golf, but given the choice, I'd rather spend a long weekend in a leper colony.

Had my experiences fetching Nachron's doodads changed me so much? Stepping across the strange borders of time and space had taught me to reconsider the crucial importance of awareness, and dismiss future expectations as the temporary decorations of an idle imagination. As you can see, I was hard at work rationalizing, in order to insulate myself against the barely possible threat of disappointment upon reuniting with Lynn.

The car radio provided no relief, as my thoughts were in a jittery balance between my nearly incomprehensible past and my totally incomprehensible future, permitting me to envy Crystal in her repose and be grateful for her company.

Winter Park was once separated from the rapidly growing city of Orlando by a thinning of the strip malls and signage that accompany suburban growth. The voracious Mouse has now pressed every nearby community into service and the quaint municipal isolation the little town once enjoyed as a seasonal refuge for snowbirds and college students was slowly eroding.

The Morris Clinic was a well-funded institution whose nominal specialty was the treatment of extreme cases of physical and mental disability. Its practical function, however, was to serve as a final, comfortable option for those whose families could no longer adequately care for them. Its location on the outskirts of town was near enough to a modern, somewhat high-end hotel whose bellmen stared discreetly but admiringly as Crystal preceded the luggage into the lobby. When I read the lips of one of the adolescent swine, I put the two five dollar bills back into my pocket to be replaced by a few ones. I was the intrepid defender of the dignity of all women apparently.

    By the time we settled ourselves into the two bedroom suite, it was too late to do anything but order room service and call it a night. I had already decided against trying to initiate contact with Lynn before morning, since I wasn't informed of her hours or her function, or even if she might be one of the inmates, so I tossed and turned in a feeble attempt to prepare myself for the most unlikely contingencies. After all this time, I was compelled to consider that a very large number of possible outcomes would be negative, ranging from simple rejection to catastrophic illness, but I was determined to see this through.

    When I heard the sound of Crystal's breakfast tray in the hall, I knew the most important day of my life was beginning. Whereas yesterday I was intent and purposeful, today I was a wreck. I couldn't eat, I couldn't focus my thoughts, and I was unable to drive a breath deeply into my lungs due to the terrible constricted feeling in my chest. My reflection in the bathroom mirror was unrecognizable, with strange haunted eyes and a nervous tic that I had never noticed before. To an onlooker, I must have seemed totally unsuitable for socializing much less romance, but there was only one person's opinion that could have discouraged me, and she could not have been aware of my proximity.

    I closed the door silently behind me and shuffled inattentively to the elevator. I thought I had pushed the lobby button, but when the door opened, I walked stupidly into the garage level and by the time I realized it, the cab had returned to an upper floor. I looked for a stairway to the lobby and found it locked at the same time that I noticed I was standing in the contents of someone's bladder. When I finally reentered the elevator to return to the lobby, I had forgotten the rehearsed speech that I hoped would draw Lynn back into my orbit.

    The strange looks I got as I paced anxiously in the atrium for the next twenty minutes included the curious stares of children whose parents brought them protectively closer, but I was not distracted. I was ready, and it was time. When the valet opened my car door, my unsteadiness must have suggested that I shouldn't be allowed behind the wheel, because he hesitated to close it again. He was clearly sensitive to potential complicity in a drunk driving incident, but I felt confident that I could negotiate the few blocks between hotel and clinic.

    I found a place to park that allowed me to look into the large windows on the side of the building as I walked to the front entrance. If I could get some hint of what I was in for, I might be able to fortify myself into an appropriate response, and I needed all the help I could get. What I saw in the third window answered many of my questions, since she seemed healthy and happy to be surrounded by several wheelchair-bound residents. As her lips moved, I could almost hear her voice inside my head, and the elderly gentleman whose hand she so tenderly held was saying something that must have made them both laugh. Of the other occupants of the room, none seemed to be watching this exchange, since their heads were variously slumped forward on their chests or awkwardly tilted sideways in one of the tragic manifestations of paralysis.

Our lives had obviously gone in such different directions that I became just a tiny bit anxious about what we might still have in common. I carried this nagging doubt with me as I walked through the front door, although I secretly believed our first touch would dispel any negative issues. A smiling receptionist whose name tag identified her as Anna came from behind a large desk to extend her hand in greeting as she uttered these surprising words: "Follow me, she's waiting for you."

I deliberately dragged my feet as I allowed myself to be led down the hall with the hope that Anna might share a bit more of what she knew. She was one of those radiant souls whose service to others seemed to impart an unnatural happiness and grace that is beyond the reach of us ordinary folks. I told her about the exchange I had seen through the window before coming in, and she responded with an indulgent smile and a pat on the back.

"Ron," she said, "no one in that room has communicated by either speech or gesture for almost eight months. Lynn's responsibility, to the extent that she is able, is to make these unlucky people as physically comfortable as possible."

I had once believed that Lynn had the sheer sexual appeal to produce impure thoughts in a 90 year old archbishop on his deathbed, but this was an entirely different matter. The exchange I believed I had observed suggested warmth and gratitude, but perhaps my agitation had caused me to see what wasn't there.

Mr. Nachron's List

She was waiting for us at the door and walked directly into my open arms. Some things feel so wonderful that it's hard to believe that someone else could feel the same palpitations, goose bumps, and short breaths that remind you how good life is. She pushed my shoulders back to a distance where she could study my eyes and told me how happy she was to see me again. I stammered some inadequate response and tried to regain my grip on her, clinging so tightly as to preclude conversation. She laughed and squirmed gracefully away, explaining that she would prefer to avoid such a public display. In light of the absence of awareness of the people sharing the room, it seemed unlikely our ardent mischief would find its way into the tabloids, but I needed a minute to regain my faculties anyway, so I refrained from chasing her down and holding her more passionately. I was out of control, you see.

Before I could work up the courage to romance her properly, she indicated that I sit beside her and be patient and she would respond to all my unasked questions.

She began: "Ron, I love you now as I loved you then. That will never change, but I can't give you the time and energy you deserve anymore. There are lots of people who depend on me, and their needs have become my inspiration, so any future we might have would be handicapped by my priorities. Please try to understand."

I protested that I could possibly relocate and maybe even get a job at the clinic. She smiled awkwardly, grabbed my hand, and said she would be thrilled to see me again in a few months and that she might reconsider my proposal.

When I started to object, she helped me out of my chair and led me slowly around the room. As we passed each individual, there was a movement or a grunt, a twitch of a finger, or an unaccountable spasm. It wasn't just weird, it was miraculous! Lynn had established relationships with a group of people who were obviously beyond the reach of traditional medicine. I imagined that her function might be to usher them seamlessly from their marginal existence to whatever might follow, but since mere survival seemed somehow unimportant in that room, Lynn, through whatever remarkable gift she possessed, offered them more. I even thought I could hear muted chuckling as we walked slowly from patient to patient, but it must have been some acoustical anomaly.

With all the amazing events of the past month, you wouldn't think an additional taste of the unbelievable would have such a profound impact on me, but I must have been mentally fragile, because I just sat down and for the first time in my life, I began to quietly cry. As her hand fell on my shoulder, a current of physical warmth overwhelmed my senses. I could feel heat swirling through my chest, wrapping around my heart, intoxicating and uplifting, in the manner perhaps that the other occupants of the room enjoyed the balm of her touch.

There was nothing left to say or do, so I could either choose to sit numbly among the others, or I could demonstrate my uniqueness by departing. I made a few sincere but forgettable comments of admiration, and then shuffled limply from the clinic and into the fading light of a Winter Park evening.

Mr. Nachron's List

On the short ride back to the hotel, I made a mental list of who or what Lynn had become or always been, and I assigned to each what I thought was an approximation of correctness.

In no particular order:

She was an angel of death or a kind of heavenly escort. 2%
She had discovered a way to heal with her personal energy. 1%
She was merely a courageous unselfish person. 1%
She was harvesting souls by deception for some evil purpose. 0%
Her nature was far beyond the reach of my limited imagination. 96%

    I was still reeling from the day's surprises as the valet patiently awaited my glacier-like movement from the car into the artificial hospitality of the hotel lobby. I wandered into the lounge, where a group of business travelers were enjoying the redundant ambience of happy hours spent away from the wife and kids. Crystal was pointedly ignoring a pair of gentlemen who were attempting to charm her with jokes recently mined from some internet source, while she studied the interior of her glass the way a microbiologist examines a fascinating slide. The girl tending bar alerted Crystal to my arrival, causing her to swivel on her stool so quickly she almost knocked one of the humorists over. She was relieved to see me, but I must have looked like I had just been mugged, since her initial appraisal turned to concern. When she reached out to touch my arm, I nearly jumped out of my shoes due to emotional instability and the pungent memory of the last time I had experienced physical contact.

When I regained my composure with the help of two, no, three vodka martinis, I obliged my extremely curious companion by recounting in detail my strange day. My mind had enough to absorb without the apparent tricks my memory was playing on me, since as well as what I knew had happened, I thought I recalled seeing a spray of flowers in a tall vase move slightly in Lynn's direction as she passed. When I described this unlikely phenomenon to Crystal, she rolled her eyes, paid our tab, and mentioned that the restaurant might be closing soon. Her pragmatism was a welcome relief from the fantastic occurrences of the recent past, so with her help I resisted the onset of regret, and melancholy was beyond my range. I knew my personality was of insufficient depth to be long affected by negative stimuli.

That night, Crystal draped one leg across my lap as we innocently (maybe another first) fell asleep on the couch. I vaguely remember dreams of angels, lepers, gunboats, and hobbits, but those fragments were not a construction of my imagination as much as the lingering memory of reality. That reality would now exclude any aspirations about a romance with Lynn, since she was really only briefly accessible, and what we shared, although life changing for me, was merely a moderately diverting (I hope) stage of growth for her. I woke up feeling confused and empty, but not yet emotionally spent.

I carefully slid out from under the tangle of Crystal's long limbs and made my way to the bathroom, where the mirror again surprised me with the resolute reflection of a determined soul who survived a beating and was ready for another fight.

I decided to see Lynn one more time before I left. I still had that Habsburg diamond, and to tell the truth, I couldn't imagine it in my ear or navel. I assumed that if it were sold at auction, it might bring enough to buy five hundred fancy wheelchairs, or pay the salaries of a couple of good nurses for twenty years, or whatever. In any event, I knew its next owner would know how to use it to the advantage of those who could best benefit.

When I arrived, Lynn was standing outside as if she already knew I would see her one last time. I left my car door open to demonstrate the brevity of my intention, and walked directly toward her with my hands in front of me; one open to grasp hers, one closed over a small box with the stone inside. She accepted my brief embrace, and as we clasped hands before parting, I passed the box into hers as seamlessly as a magician might have. In order not to prolong and thus devalue that final exchange, I looked into her amazing eyes one last time and turned to leave, feeling the supernatural warmth of her stare on my back as I walked away.

That damned stone must have weighed more than I thought since I now felt a hundred pounds lighter, or perhaps it was the elation that a performer of a selfless act is entitled to. I couldn't say, since my experience with that sensation was so limited, but I felt a healthy sense of completion as that phase of my life ended.

In the cathartic state that I basked in as I drove back to the hotel, I made another decision. If it felt so good to help those other people, maybe it wouldn't be such a bad idea to include Crystal among my beneficiaries. She could have compromised her values a hundred times by settling for a comfortable life as the wife of a corrupt attorney or a philandering neurosurgeon, but she chose to remain stubbornly single, living in a tiny apartment without the Rolex and the expensive shoes you would expect to see under legs like hers. She never stole from the owner of the bar, nor did she pander to drunken patrons, but she managed an adequate existence with simple competency and selective charm. In short, she was the ideal candidate for a $50,000 tip.

    We packed and left the hotel after a quiet breakfast, during which I caught Crystal studying me frequently for signs of damage, emotional or otherwise. I waited until we were on the turnpike heading south before I sprung my little surprise on her. I told her everything that had happened, finishing with my notion to split the money Nachron had given me with her. She gradually went from disbelief to refusal to guarded consideration before she arrived, about an hour later, at this counterproposal. She consented to accept my offer only if we could pool our $100,000 as a down payment on a condo. This may all seem a little hasty for the traditional taste, but I had no dream to invest in the stock market or buy a CD, so it made perfect sense. Moreover, I was as flattered by Crystal's invitation to share that part of her life as she was impressed by the generosity of sharing my wealth.

    Without each other knowing, we had both decided that in the event of some unanticipated awkwardness, either of us would walk away, leaving the property without encumbrance to the other. We were alike in so many ways, I was more than a little surprised we hadn't embarked on a course like this even sooner. Sometimes, one may hope, successes are the consequence of circumstances beyond our ability to design. As I looked across the car to her profile, backlit by the afternoon sun, I felt very, very lucky.

 I woke Crystal with the centrifugal force created by a quick trip around the Fort Lauderdale exit ramp. She responded by mumbling something about food, then squirming against the seat belt into a new position to sleep. This was her way of assigning me the task of choosing the appropriate setting for ending this phase of my life and starting another, and I was equal to the task.

 If you had to create a symbolic event to celebrate rebirth, you would probably agree that this is best done with mountains of spicy food and some long-neck Coronas, so we spent the next three hours deliberately avoiding potentially painful subjects while enjoying the cuisine and hospitality of the Casa Maya in Hillsboro Beach. By the end of the night, the owner and two of the waitresses had joined us for tequilas and a lot of laughing.

 It was late, so Crystal drove us back to her place, where the couch was by now familiar. She would always throw a pillow from her own bed to me as I settled in, and that night I pushed it into my face and breathed the borrowed scents of her hair and neck. Is that weird? Moments later, I saw her through the partially open bedroom door as she caught me enjoying her pillow. She had an odd expression on her face for a moment, but it twisted into a little smile as she turned her light out.

The next morning, I woke up to find her at the opposite end of the couch reading the newspaper. She was wearing the tee shirt she had slept in and was sitting on her legs not really paying attention to her feet, which were both touching my own. This was a nice way to wake up, but it was confusing to assess the significance of this apparent familiarity. Was it like holding hands with your sister or did it mean something else? The impulse that I did not respond to was to grab her feet and pull them up toward me so our bodies would be against one another. This not only produced the possibility of being kicked in the head by a startled Crystal, it required that I somehow justify the awkward configuration of her laying face up on top of me with her feet in my face. The deciding factor in this peculiar rumination was that the weight of her body on my bladder might produce a decidedly unromantic outcome. Who was I kidding? We're just pals.

"Good morning Ron. What the hell are you thinking about with your face all scrunched up like that?"

"Never look for birds of this year in the nests of the last"
Miguel de Cervantes

TWENTY-NINE

Another Mystery

Although we felt no sense of obligation to bring Albert Nachron up to date about our trip, we had all been through so much together that Crystal and I wanted to share the end of the story with him. We had become almost like family; a very odd family. The short ride to Las Olas was unremarkable and the weather was balmy and typical of late summer, but the normalcy of the morning was about to vanish along with our hopes of a reunion.

We left the car with the valet and presented ourselves at the reception desk. I guess I shouldn't have been too surprised that the attendant didn't recognize me since my comings and goings through the front door were relatively infrequent, but this was the same guy who was so recently dazzled by my companion that he admitted her without the required screening. My request to ring up Nachron's apartment was met with a curious response. The attendant, now flanked by the security guard, informed us that there was no tenant with that name currently in residence, and furthermore that his apartment had been vacant for some time.

"What about my stuff?" I blurted. "What about his stuff?"

The security guard noticeably stiffened as I raised my voice, but the attendant patiently explained that the apartment's last tenant had put his furniture and personal effects in storage.

"If you would like to speak to the building manager, he's not available today, but I can give you the phone number of his office."

Crystal and I shared puzzled looks and then walked a few feet from the desk, where I implored her to assure me that if I were crazy, she would agree to be crazy with me.

"Not so loud, Ron," she whispered "even most crazy people know it's a bad idea to let everybody else know it."

There were people going through the lobby during the course of our discussion, variously on their way in or out to a waiting car. I started approaching them to ask about any recollection they might have had regarding our unique looking friend, which was the last straw for the security guard. Since Crystal was closer to him then I was, he grabbed her roughly by the arm, which was foolish for two reasons. I was the one causing most of the disturbance in the lobby, and seeing this clearly improper treatment of my friend, I was quickly deciding between either breaking his arm or merely dislocating it. Crystal, not particularly troubled by the guard's grip on her, saw what was about to happen and snarled a warning at both of us. He immediately released her and I forgot what I was planning as we simultaneously reacted to her venomous tone. The guard, who had probably never met anybody like Crystal, walked to my side and said in a very quiet voice: "Dude you gotta get her out of here." Where had I heard something like that before?

Once outside, she lectured me; "If I hadn't put my foot down in there, that may have escalated into something that would've made it a lot trickier to get rid of the 'crazy' label."

She was right of course, but she should also have realized that we couldn't possibly walk away as if nothing unusual had happened. Since together we had enough tangible evidence to eliminate the possibility that two people suffered an identical long term delusion, we decided to do a little detective work on our own.

Crystal's boss called to make sure she would be behind the bar that night, so I told her I'd meet her later in order to make a list of places to look for the answers we needed. Talking to waiters at nearby restaurants and clerks at some of the local stores seemed like a good start, so we mapped out a five block area of places where Nachron might have shopped. When I left Murray's early for Crystal's apartment, I promised to let her sleep until lunchtime, when we would begin to execute our plan in earnest.

In the course of the next day's project, we consumed coffees, teas and a couple of croque monsieurs without adding to what we knew about Nachron's mysterious disappearance. By late afternoon it seemed unlikely that enlarging our five block search area would improve our chances, so we went to the library instead. We sat at adjoining computers until one of the soft-voiced employees told us we could return in the morning, but the library would be open for only ten more minutes.

So far we had little to encourage us, but during the late afternoon of the following day, before Crystal had given up to get ready for work, we stumbled onto something interesting among some old tax records. After two hours studying city and county documents, I learned that a small commercial building with the same Las Olas address had been owned by a fellow named Alvin Nachron, who had apparently perished in a fire that consumed the structure before the United States entered World War II.

A few decades earlier, there was a gentleman with the coincidentally similar name of Nackern, who was known to have conducted a lively trade on the New River with enterprising Native Americans. As near as I could judge, he ran his business in exactly the same location as the twenty-first century Nachron's apartment building. The trail went cold in Broward County, but on a hunch and with Crystal's help, I did a comprehensive search of Florida's historical records, with the result being the discovery of a single relevant transcribed document. It was from St. Augustine and handwritten in Spanish, so it took us quite a while to learn that there was a minor functionary of the Crown of Spain whose partially smudged name was Alberto Nac_____. It might seem that at that point my imagination was beginning to supplant the spirit of scholarly inquiry, and to tell the truth, as tantalizing as this information was, it brought us no closer to our twin goals of finding Albert and putting our many doubts to rest.

Mike Corbett

"Time is a brisk wind, for each hour it brings something new...but who can understand and measure its sharp breath, its mystery and its design."   Paracelsus

THIRTY

Night

If you asked somebody in Bozeman or Gstaad what fresh air feels like, he might describe some uncontaminated cold breeze recently scrubbed by mountain pines or clear Alpine streams. Granted, that's excellent air, but I prefer something totally different. For eight months a year, hot air is drawn upward from the African Continent and rises over the Atlantic, swirling and gusting across the ocean to arrive on North America's east coast. This air is neither thin nor cool so not everyone praises it, but it has been purified by its long trip within the prevailing southeasterly flow and it rewards the lungs and skin with its own virtues.

This cottony humid substance is best enjoyed when it comes ashore at between ten and twenty knots on a moonlit night, lightly spiced by the salt from wave tops and accompanied by the sounds every shoreline offers. People who think they simply like the beach are ignorant of the narcotic properties that prolonged exposure to that atmosphere will produce, but it doesn't really matter whether you are aware of it. You have been seduced.

I bet I've walked to the end of Anglin's pier thousands of times, and when I get to the tee, I survey the 180 degrees of horizon like the skipper of an eighteenth century sailing vessel. It's rarely crowded when I go, so I can let my eyes glaze over and dream unlikely dreams if I want. Or I can scream into the wind. The ocean doesn't care about my frustration.

That night, I didn't go all the way to the end. I was lying on my stomach about halfway out to the tee with my head and arms over the edge of the planking looking for fish that like encrusted pilings and shadows. It was one o'clock in the morning and Crystal was at home with our daughter Jenny, who seems to prefer Mahler to Green Day although she's not quite eleven months old. The three of us are happy and blessed with good health so I have no reason to be restless, but I haven't slept very well for some time. Crystal and I watch Jenny nod off, I read in bed for a while listening for the moment when I know they're both asleep, then I sneak quietly out the front door. We live so close to the pier that my family has become tolerant of my nocturnal trips, and if Crystal opened a window and yelled my name, I could be beside them in ninety seconds.

Fishing is the perfect activity for keeping the hands and eyes busy while permitting the mind to wander into greater depths. Serious fishermen will argue that you can only maximize results with all of your attention riveted on the objective, but once you have acquired a sense of the methodical array of considerations that may be required to fool a fish, you can function in a reasonably effective manner without trying to think like one. If you rely on your reflexes to respond without overreacting, you can reflect on Euclid or Newton with only a small sacrifice of efficiency. Save some part of your awareness to consider the startling array of marine life that you can see when the water's clear. Stingrays, sharks, tarpon and rays will present themselves almost any summer night, and individuals and schools of smaller species thrive in the friendly environment of pier and reef.

    At that hour on a weekday most of the noisy people have gone home, and the fish seem to lose their skittishness when they can't hear lots of commotion above them. From behind a piling, a moonfish appeared, not one of those fancy extinct ones, just a single garden-variety moonfish, turning into the current and rotating so I could see his broad angular shape.

    Even on my stomach with my face down, I would not have thought it possible for someone to sneak up on me. In the relative silence and darkness, you can enjoy a state of hyper-awareness that may be a throwback to a time when hunting and survival demanded it. That's why I was so surprised by a familiar voice directly above me wishing me a pleasant evening.

    On the shimmering side of the moonfish below, I briefly saw what I thought was the smiling image of my old friend. You may think that this hallucination was a consequence of spending too much time with blood running to my head as I fished, or that it may have been the concussion I suffered as a result of hitting my head on the pier's lower railing, but being unconscious is not like being insane. As I peeled myself from the planks and dizzily began to gather my equipment, I noticed something incongruous. I never leave a tackle box open for many reasons I will not bore you with, but there it was, wide open with nothing missing that I could see. There was one small addition, however. There, on the top tray, was that tiny Habsburg purse, with a note announcing that it was a present from an old friend to our daughter Jenny on her first birthday.

"There is nothing in the whole world which abides. All things are in a state of ebb and flow, and every shadow passes away. Even time itself, like a river, is constantly gliding away."   Ovid

THIRTY-ONE

The Beginning

Our sun has sufficient fuel to burn at or near current intensity for a few billion more years, and although some stars with greater mass are destined to expire with a flourish, we should not expect anything as ostentatious as a supernova. Long before the United States is able to repay its enormous debt to the Chinese, our planet's atmosphere will be cooked away and all recognizable life will have vanished from its surface. Earth may seem like a more scorched version of today's Mars.

What evidence of our existence will remain? Perhaps in another galaxy or even another dimension, we may find Tao or Nirvana. Heaven may not be necessary, but I have recently been allowing myself to believe otherwise.

When Jennifer was old enough to realize she couldn't see as well as the other kids, I tried to explain to her that her musical talent was more than compensation for her physical handicap. She just cried. That night, I spent sleeplessly agonizing over her condition, but I believe that long after the sun cools, Jennifer will be making people cry somewhere by playing her violin for them. That hope is heaven enough for me.

BIBLIOGRAPHY

Naval letters from the Civil War; a private collection.

Richard P. Feynman. "Surely You're Joking Mr. Feynman". ©1985 By Richard P. Feynman and Ralph Leighton.

ABOUT THE AUTHOR

MIKE CORBETT was born in Louisville Kentucky. He was raised in Fort Lauderdale Florida, and went to college and graduate school at Rollins College in Winter Park Florida. He is the author of *Backgammon Problems (2007)* and *Laughter of the Damned (2009)*.

Made in the USA
Charleston, SC
16 November 2011